# Fractured State

By: Walter Duke Harris, M.D.

## Editor's Note:

The author of this story possessed a unique combination of self-drive and selflessness. He embodied what it is to be a patriot; to give of one's time and expertise to strengthen their community.

Motivated by the fear of digging ditches his whole life in the arid fields of his hometown of Texarkana, Arkansas he fulfilled his dream of using the gifts God had given him by becoming a doctor. His love of family, profession and country drove much of his existence. Like most Americans he possessed an optimistic attitude with a healthy dose of cynicism that he consciously kept in check.

He often talked about writing a book when he retired. This concept often buried in today's fast-paced world of sensationalism is reflected in the main character of his story—duty first, play later. When that retirement day arrived, he embarked on his new dream. Like so many blessings bestowed and, yet, uncounted, he was granted one year to bring that dream to completion before leaving this world. He succeeded.

He desired to author a story that would offer insight into his occupation while entertaining people. This is that story.

Prologue

Near the end of the Bronze Age, just before men learned to make more powerful weapons from iron, legend tells that the gods created the most beautiful of women. Helen, it is said, came into being in Sparta but was later taken to Troy. That was reason enough to start a war. A siege raged outside the walls of that great city for ten years, and many brave warriors died before their time.

Why the gods of old would send only one perfect woman to earth is a quandary that has been debated by philosophers through the ages.

If she were meant to be a "thank you" gift to man for his good deeds, as some say, then maybe they should have considered giving us something we could have used like penicillin or the polio vaccine.

If she were meant to be fought over, causing men to be killed in a war as a means to help control the overpopulated and crowded conditions of the cities, as other scholars maintain, then possibly something from the contraceptive line of products would have caused fewer headaches and premature deaths.

If the gods were just bored and looking for something to occupy their time, as a third faction claims, perhaps they should have just picked up a good book.

Chapter One

It was the third trimester of another Washington winter. The membranes that held the birth of spring were stretched thin, bulging tightly near rupture, while each new blast of snow and sleet only served to increase the misery. The failure of the sun became more painful with every freezing day. It was that nearly intolerable part of the year when even the stark, lifeless branches overhead struggled to conceal their buds. The trees had learned. It was the dark time for patient waiting. The season for change would come, but it could not be hurried.

Only a few foot-travelers were about on the cold, late Friday afternoon, trudging through the snow to the safety of their warm cocoons. The weather was fit for only the most driven of men and the most desperate of beasts, but the girl in the pink parka stood out from her fellow sojourners. She levitated up the four steps to her new front door, tried to manage the small bag of groceries she carried as she fumbled with her key and entered the small apartment. Anxious and eager, she had left her cell phone behind on her couch and its chime was fading. In a rush, she tossed the bag of groceries on a chair, threw her coat on the floor and ran to the phone. Too late. She sighed and plopped down to listen to the two messages.

The first one was from the cable company trying to set an appointment to hook up her connection. The second was from a local wireless carrier offering better service at a special introductory rate for first time subscribers. She should call them back during business hours on Monday.

Sitting there on the sofa, she looked around and felt a certain pride. Her coat was on the floor and the groceries were spilled in a chair, but this was her very own apartment. It was unshared, private, and she could do as she pleased and answer to no one. Jane, as she would come to be known, was changing. She was in control now, and would never again wait for someone else to tell her how to lead her life.

After starting the water in the bathtub, Jane arranged the contents of the little sack of groceries on the shelves in the small kitchen cabinet. The space was rather limited, but she didn't need much room. She would not be eating in very often; instead, Jane would be dining out in expensive candlelit restaurants, and certainly not alone. There would be polished silver, glittering crystal and fresh scented flowers on the starched linen, but she would be the centerpiece of the table.

Back in her Southern hometown, Jane was the mousy, overlooked girl from Marketing Research in the only large company around, a too thin waif with an unsightly Roman nose. The handicap had always been present, but over the last two years, the more she looked, the uglier her nose became.

Jane was a very smart girl. If the company she worked for had listened to her, it would not have needed to down-size. She'd learned from her marketing experience that appearance and presentation were everything. The nose had to be fixed. It wasn't cancer. It was worse. It was ugly. And, while she was at it, there might be a few other things about her body that could be perfected. "Added value", as they say. She'd seen how the men looked at the other women in tighter blouses. They got the promotions that she deserved.

A bargain hunter by nature, Jane used the vast power of the internet for her shopping pleasure. She looked at hundreds of sites for plastic surgery, and a comparison of local doctors' fees with the cost of medical tourism revealed an amazing conclusion. She was on the right track. A plan was forming.

After days of searching online, reading testimonials and comparing before and after photographs, she was convinced. She could afford not only the perfect nose, but also a breast-enhancement procedure and a resort vacation overseas. Imperial Medical Tours was the way to go.

The downsizing at work would not affect her because she had acted first. She had borrowed some money from her credit card account, left the mundane job and moved to D.C. Jane had barely settled into her new apartment before she boarded a plane for the sunny Mediterranean.

She flew all night over the ocean and most of Europe before a personal travel escort met her and a group of twenty or so other tourists at the airport. After customs and clearance, the escort was thoughtful enough to collect their passports for safe-keeping.

He also collected their cell phones, since they might interfere with the monitors in the hospital. Besides, the signal was so weak they would be of no use.

After a short bus ride, Jane was at the admissions desk of a small, clean hospital in the warm perfumed air of an exotic foreign country that she had previously only read about and seen pictured in the glossy travel magazines. Later that afternoon, she met a professional, personable, American plastic surgeon named Dr. Moore. He reviewed her medical history and performed a thorough examination. He then asked about her expectations as he made a sketch of her face.

"Does this look like what you had in mind for the result of your nose?"

"Why yes, maybe even a little smaller," she said. "How did you know?"

"I think this would complement your features well. You're a very pretty girl," he said.

He continued talking as he began to mark her chest with a skin pencil. "As far as size is concerned, we don't want to go too large. I would suggest about a 350 cc implant on each side."

"How big do they come?"

"Well, they come up to 700, but with your frame, I certainly wouldn't recommend that."

"How about 550?" she said.

He looked and thought and drew some more before he finally said, "Yes, that would do nicely. We could do that, if you're sure. Imperial Medical brings in its own implants," he continued, "Same silicone-gel or saline used all over the world, FDA approved. Perfectly safe."

Waking up after her surgery, Jane did not even remember being taken into the operating room. She did recall coming around some in recovery. She was frightened, and she couldn't catch her breath for a minute until they took that tube out. There was some discomfort later, but she could have all the pain medicine she wanted. When the dressings were changed on the following day, she was thrilled. Even with the bruising and the swelling, she could tell she would be beautiful. The worst part was the sore throat and raspy voice from the tube that had been in her windpipe during the procedure.

After a day or two in the hospital, she and the rest of her group were taken to the resort to relax and recover. There she met a diverse mix of post-op patients. The ones who had come for cosmetic procedures were all pleased and excited, while the ones who had had their joints replaced were grateful just to be free of pain. There were three people who had been there before and had both types of surgery, and also several dental patients who could not wait to smile and show off their new gleaming implants.

While the hotel wasn't exactly five-star, it was well kept and comfortable. There was no pool, but there was a nice beach with plenty of warm sunshine overlooking an idyllic azure sea. There were no demands, and Jane kept to herself--at least for now, before long the world would experience the new Jane.

The ace bandages that encircled her chest, under her arms and around her upper back, were a bit of a hindrance. They kept the sun away from those areas and were itchy in the warm climate, but it would soon be worth it. The rest of her body became a beautiful golden brown just like in the brochure. The bruising about her nose and face gradually faded as the sun worked its magic. After a week of relaxation, the trip back home seemed very short indeed.

When she returned to her apartment she dropped her luggage on the floor and headed for a refreshing bath. She emerged from the tub and dried herself, revealing the results of her pilgrimage. The value of modern cosmetic surgery was outstanding—well worth the investment. She almost didn't recognize her own image. More beautiful than Helen of Troy, like the ads had promised.

This was her city now but she didn't know anyone in it, yet. Her job didn't start for another week. Meanwhile, she had decided for her first real outing to go to the small, upscale club she'd passed on the way home from the store.

After finishing her hair and make-up for the occasion, she began to think about what she'd wear: something revealing, but not too revealing. She wanted to leave a little to the imagination with her new figure, but nothing she owned would require too much imagination. She decided that the new blue dress was the perfect choice for the night. She almost laughed out loud when she dreamt about how this was D.C.; while Senator Left might work in one of the big white buildings downtown, the honorable Mr. Right might already be waiting for her in the bar.

The woman that looked back from the mirror was irresistible. *This would be like baiting with goldfish: catch your limit, don't mess with the little ones, but keep the really big boys in the live well.* A spritz of the fine French perfume, duty free of course, in all the right places, and she was ready for the evening. She put on her coat and the boots with the three-inch heels and was out the door.

The city was darker than she liked when traveling alone, but she was only going a few blocks. She decided to walk. After only a short distance, she felt, maybe more than heard, a noise from behind. *Was someone watching? Probably.* She would have to get used to that. While she had been shopping for groceries earlier she had noticed that men really were watching her. With her new full figure and her perfect nose, the glances had become second looks, and the second looks had become stares.

*Again, that feeling, that sound, maybe from ahead, maybe from behind; movie stars put up with this all the time.* She would need to learn how to peer down her small graceful nose at her new admirers, but that would take some practice. For now she tossed her head and didn't bother to turn. She just kept walking through the snow beside the buildings toward the lights in front of her. Let them look all they wanted; she would decide who could touch. Then time stopped.

The last thing Jane felt was intolerable panic as something lifted her body from the ground. A vise tightened around her throat. Her arms flailed helplessly at the unseen crushing force. The pressure increased in her windpipe like it had with the tube in the Recovery Room. No matter how desperately she struggled, she couldn't get any precious air to come into her lungs. They were bursting; she could not even cry out for help.

The final sound in the quiet darkness of the cold night was the sickening crunch of the hyoid bone as it exploded inside the front of her small pretty neck. While her unseen attacker eased her body to the ground, there was neither enough breath nor enough time to recognize that she was not in control. Jane's twenty-eighth spring would never come. She had changed and could never go back. She had become Jane Doe.

Chapter Two

The troublesome wintry mix was falling on the windshield just hard enough to require an annoying manual sweep as the blades staggered back and forth. A little more snow and the wipers could be placed on "auto." A little less and they could lie back down in their warm beds on the hood and maybe get some rest.

That in-between start and stop action matched the mood of the driver, John Christopher Thomas, MD, whose mindset was closer to the pull-the-covers-back-over-your-head stage. JC, as most of his friends called him, was on his way to the hospital at 6:30 in the morning on Saturday, staring right at forty-eight straight hours of availability for orthopaedic emergency calls. That would be followed by a ten-to-twelve hour regular workday on Monday. He almost always managed to get some sleep during the on-call weekend, but he couldn't count on it. He couldn't really count on much of anything, besides just reacting and trying to make it through.

He had to go in early. There were patients waiting to be discharged, and the hospital needed to clean their rooms to get ready for the next wave. Beds were scarce all over town during flu season, but JC's exact time of arrival was not minute-to-minute urgent. He took a sip from the Styrofoam cup. It was lukewarm at best, strong and bitter, but the coffee wasn't working very well this morning. He was stalling, dragging his feet by taking a winding departure from his usual straight route into the city to work.

Even though he'd lived in the Washington area for years, he still hadn't seen all the grand office buildings and statues. Sometimes the architecture of the huge government structures, the memorials and what they stood for, really inspired him, but it wasn't helping this morning. With the low clouds and the spitting snow, he couldn't even see the five hundred fifty-five foot monument to the Father of the Country. They'd probably had to camouflage it during the night for security reasons.

Many things had changed in this country and the radical extremists had caused a lot of trouble in the world. What kinds of minds could they possibly have to dream up the things they had tried? Who thought up things like learning to fly giant aircraft and then crashing it into the towers of commerce, blowing up a government building with a truck load of fertilizer, poisoning a guy in London with alpha radiation, or trying to light a pair of shoes over the Atlantic, for God's sake? More importantly, what kinds of imaginations did the people who were trying to protect us have to have just to keep up? Well, at least he didn't have to worry about it except to work and pay his taxes, which were due next month. He'd have to get out in the garage and start looking for all that IRS paperwork pretty soon, but not this week. He had enough to do.

There was one thing he had resolved a few years earlier. Like many Americans, the terrorist acts would not get to him; he would not be intimidated. It would be a cold day in Hades across the River Styx before murdering fanatics would force him to change his behavior.

JC was almost always in a good mood, but today he was really feeling sorry for himself. That didn't happen often enough for him to even recognize the emotion. It was almost always self-healing. Usually the cure came before the diagnosis was confirmed. The treatment was to get busy and solve someone else's problem while forgetting his. Such is the beauty of orthopaedic surgery.

Most of the time in the bone and joint business people are broken and hurt. He fixed them, and could see it on an X-ray right away. People got well and were grateful, and that made him feel good. In some other fields of medicine, say allergy or psychiatry, patients get better slowly, but seldom all the way. There is no real closure.

On the other hand, those specialists were probably still home in bed with their spouses on a snowy Saturday morning. Or perhaps they were sitting in front of the DVD with their children watching a purple dinosaur who was always in a good mood—obviously the result of one of the newer antidepressant medications and apparently worth the noticeable side effects to the

8

skin pigment.

JC had no immediate plans and not much to look forward to when a police car, lights flashing, sped past going the other direction. In fact, JC had no intermediate nor long term plans either as the warning beep from the dashboard taunted him: "Low Fuel Level."

A second car blazed in the opposite lane and this time the siren drew his attention. He traveled another mile or two and the crime scene van, just like the ones on television, approached. At least he wasn't the only one going in to work early on this bleak winter morning.

A black Ford with the stick-on red bubble flashing from the roof followed at some distance and was the last of the convoy. As they disappeared in the rear view, JC realized that someone back there was already having a lot worse day than he possibly would.

He had been driving down "K Street" when he remembered there was a service station one block over toward "M". As he turned onto the intervening road looking for gas, the temperature had dropped several degrees and his car spun just a bit on the icy pavement. It would take a while before he understood that "L" was starting to freeze over.

\*\*\*\*\*\*\*\*\*\*\*\*\*\*\*\*\*

After the last police car traveled another mile or so, it came to a stop near the crime scene tape. Chief Investigator Murray Lane parked his Crown Victoria and surveyed the area around the third Jane Doe to be found in the area over the last ten days.

Outside, a swarm of detectives and people from forensics were spilling in and out of the narrow alley where the body had been discovered. On either side were office buildings, five and six stories high, which would be buzzing during the week but were vacant on Saturday and Sunday. There were thousands of people living within a six-block radius, and this was not considered one of the "bad" parts of town, although it seemed someone was trying to change that image.

The Chief sneezed and blew his reddened nose one more time while still in the privacy of his vehicle. He'd been fighting this

9

cold for over a week now. Like most of the community, he was not winning—it was a tie at best. The Chief felt terrible and thought that it might be the flu. He'd had all the shots, but they were always coming up with new strains. It was with some effort that he dragged his middle-aged body out of the car into the cold gray morning, coughing and sneezing as his assistants, Tim and LB approached. LB, as she liked to be called, was a thoughtful, well-organized young woman who, given some time, would be a very good detective. She was wearing practical brown snow boots and a down parka with a hood.

Tim, the younger of the two, was almost running to meet the Chief, expensive coffee sloshing out of the paper cup bearing a familiar logo and falling onto his reptile leather loafers. *He probably should have kept the lid on*, The Chief thought. *Wasn't that a law in California? Or should he switch to decaf?*

The Chief thought *Good Morning* really seemed out of place, so he simply asked, "What have you got for me so far?"

"First and foremost, Chief, this one is really nasty," Tim said. "This time I think we've got a true serial killer working - big time!"

*That's the bottom line*, the Chief thought. *Two worn out phrases in one breath. You've got to be kidding.*

"I swear, a couple of tourists were out jogging, even with the bad weather," Tim continued, "came by the alley, and noticed a brand new boot lying at the entrance. They spotted the second boot a little farther in and then they saw the body, what's left of it, back here behind the trash cans. Heck of a shock for them. They're back at the hotel, probably packing to leave town."

Tim's words tumbled on. "This one is even worse than the other two. The guy must really be nuts. Probably lives near the area and stalks his victims. He's a mixed up sexual pervert, mutilating these girls something terrible and taking body parts for souvenirs. Most likely a white male psychopath who'll continue killing until he's caught. He'll make some mistakes pretty soon and we'll have this one all wrapped up before it gets out of hand."

The Chief thought, *it was already out of hand, but if Tim had this one nearly solved, why did they need him? Couldn't he just take some aspirin and go back to bed? He'd simply watch the*

10

*trial on TV.*

While the Chief fed off the energy and enthusiasm of the young people, they did need to be tempered with some experience, and as the Chief of Homicide for D.C. Metro, he certainly had plenty of that. Start with sniper attacks, missing interns with political connections and numerous drug-related deaths. Add some exposure to the terrorist actions at the Pentagon and the biological weapons cases at the post office. Throw in a few spouses for life insurance and love triangles gone sour. Heap on a generous portion of shady business deals or arguments over nothing, and the Chief had a world of experience. Like a Chinese buffet, life had given him a taste of everything and he was uncomfortably stuffed, but the cooks just kept working the line.

"Tim, why don't you tell me a little about the people who found her?"

"Well, Chief, I talked to them at length. They're from the Midwest, Ohio I think, a married couple here for a convention. They seemed innocent enough to me. I really don't think they had any connection to the victim, if that's what you're thinking. They saw the body back in the alley and called 911 on their cell phone. They were still sitting out here in the street when I drove up."

He paused for a sip. It definitely wasn't decaf.

"We took a lot of notes. They were pretty rattled, so I let them go on back to their hotel after I got them calmed down a little bit. Of course, I got their names and personal data if you want to talk with them again."

"No, let's save that for later. Sounds like you did a pretty good job."

The police photographers were wrapping up their business and the crime scene investigators had finished with the first phase of their work. The press and TV people were gathered some distance away, but were not allowed to directly observe the scene in the alley as the Chief, Tim and LB walked over to look at the third body.

Even though he'd been in the military and had seen brutal death on the battlefield and many, many times on this job, he'd never gotten completely used to it. If he ever did, he thought he should probably move on up to Administration. This was one of the worst he had seen.

The first Jane Doe was found half-clothed with portions of her breasts slashed off and taken from the scene. There were multiple incisions in her abdomen and no attempt to hide her body. The second was missing the whole front of her chest and her hands had been removed. The face and torso were butchered beyond recognition.

This third girl's corpse was even more startling and bizarre. Her blue dress was unzipped and gathered around her waist. Her breasts were completely removed down through the muscles that covered the rib cage. Her hands had been amputated through the joints of her wrists and taken away. Like the other two, she was lying on her back with her legs spread apart. The bloody ends of her forearms were folded across her mutilated trunk and there were large lacerations throughout her abdomen.

Even more horrible and dramatic, unlike the other victims, her neck had been completely cut through. The head and face, along with the entire front of her chest and hands, were nowhere to be found: just the bloody ends of the arteries, windpipe and spinal cord lying on top of a small pool of dark blood.

They would await forensic verification, but it looked like this butchery had been accomplished in the same slashing manner used on the first two women. Both boots had come off, probably when she was pulled from the street into the alley as the drag marks indicated. Through the sheer hose he could see the perfectly polished toenails of a young woman who took pride in her appearance. Her underwear, purse and any jewelry she might have been wearing were all missing.

Tim indicated there had been no evidence of a struggle. The killer must have gotten very close before he had struck. He thought maybe they had known each other. Mercifully, the blood patterns indicated that she had probably died before she was mutilated. At least the heart had stopped pumping, but the exact manner of death was yet to be determined.

There was no sign of blood out on the street and with the new snow and slush, no obvious traces of the killer remained. There were no known witnesses, no weapon was found at the scene, and no one had come forward with any additional information.

This killer—all the evidence indicated it was the same one from the first two cases—seemed to be getting bolder and more brazen, learning as he continued his brutal spree. They might have a chance with the other two, but this girl would be very difficult to ID and it would take a lot of luck from an outside source to get a name on her anytime soon.

She had probably been attacked right out on the open street. Trace evidence could be mingled from all the other people passing this way and was unlikely to be of any value. The removed parts could easily be destroyed or disposed of in a city like this and possibly never found. The torso would have been more difficult to hide, but why would that be necessary? Virtually all manner of obvious identification had been removed. And, as Tim had observed, part of the game, it seemed, was the posing of bodies and resulting shock of this brutality, the taunting of the police and bringing fear to the public.

The forensics team might be able to develop some DNA if the girl hid some of her killer's fluids or tissue inside her body. That could help if there were some previous samples in the database, but the Chief had a sick feeling in his gut that this one had never been in the system before. The other two women had not yielded any traces of their attacker. It would take a lot of old fashion police work to catch this monster. The dress and boots might offer some clue to her past, but that was a long shot at best.

The Chief and LB continued to study what little remained of this one--no tattoos, no scars, no needle tracks. It was just somebody's precious little girl filled with the dreams of the young, only a little older than his own daughters. Now she was so lifeless and cold that even the snow that had fallen on her during the night blanketed her. It didn't melt.

He pulled on the shoe covers offered by LB and advanced a step closer.

The medical examiner acknowledged him with, "Hello, Murray. Please watch your step."

"Good morning, doc," he said. "Mind if I look over your shoulder from here?"

"No, but we're getting ready to turn her. You should be

okay where you are."

The first victim was a rather small, pale woman and the second was a dark-skinned, middle-aged lady. As she was turned, he noticed the current victim was a young woman of average build with a peculiar suntan pattern. The panty area had been protected from the rays and was starkly white in color; the front of the chest was missing, but the upper back and sides were also pale. The remainder of the corpse, even the tops of the shoulders, had a golden-brown color with no strap marks.

"I wonder how she would get that particular tan pattern?" the Chief said.

"Well, wearing a tube top and bikini bottom could account for it," LB said before Tim interrupted.

"Dead of winter? Probably going to a tanning salon. We should check all those in the area."

"Could be from out of town," LB observed.

"What do we know about the time of death?" the Chief said, including Tim in the discussion.

"With the cold weather and no wind, the techs estimate from the core body temp sometime between eight and midnight last night, about the same time of day as the others. They say that the weather does make it a bit harder to be dead on. The killer probably works daytimes and does his hunting at night. We'll catch this guy soon; we just have to get into his head."

The Chief was pretty sure that he didn't want to be in this monster's head, and, if his young assistant ever got there, he hoped he wouldn't stay for very long.

"Pretty sharp straight cuts and right between the bones of the neck," Tim said as he bent over the corpse. "He musta' known what he was doing. I'll bet he had some experience. Maybe a surgeon, like Jack the Ripper."

"Hmmm ... " the Chief said.

"Do you want us to talk to the press?" Tim said.

"No, sounds like you've got enough to do. LB, why don't you take a few of the men and start canvassing the neighborhood? See if anybody saw anything, and I'll talk to the press."

The Chief had three children of his own. There was a fine line between duty to warn and creating a public panic. Best to speak the truth and nothing but the truth. Well, maybe not the whole truth, he thought as he stepped toward the dueling microphones and cameras.

"Another woman's body has been found. There is no direct link to other open cases at this time ... ongoing investigation ... anyone with knowledge about this please come forward. Take all reasonable precautions ... try to stay in public places ... travel in groups in well-lit areas ... avoid suspicious persons. We'll update you as more becomes known."

He carefully avoided the usual closing, "Any questions?" as he turned and headed for the car before he started sneezing again. The handkerchief he took from his pocket in some ways resembled a small white flag, and he wondered if some of that hot Chinese mustard might prevent his sinus cavities from their impending rupture.

Chapter Three

The most dangerous species of animal, a hardened powerful man of no conscience, crouched on the basement floor of a brownstone apartment. He was encapsulated and secure like a spore buried underground in the rotting soil. The creature that had shed his skin and emerged from another place halfway around the world was now only four miles from the National Mall in the District called Columbia. The tarnished numbers nailed beside the front door read 2109 and the badly patched street in front of his building was lined with dull, unreliable cars. He was only a few blocks removed from a spray-painted dirty gray canvas of five story towers for public housing.

The man had taken a twisted, serpentine path back to his lair, occasionally stopping to turn and retrace his steps. He had been careful to avoid the popular tourist areas where the watchful eyes of security cameras and heavy traffic threatened even during the cold nighttime hours. Along the way he had disposed of the unwanted remains of his night's work, a meal for the vermin, in several of the metal dumpsters that lined the back of the dark buildings. He carried the choicest pieces with him in airtight plastic containers secure inside his pack.

15

The man was not afraid to travel on foot through the bleak neighborhoods, where only an occasional delivery vehicle ventured. He was armed with a large sharp knife and feared no one. There were many places to dispose of small sacks of garbage, and in the big city, even if some of the items were to be discovered, the people who slept in the streets would not alert the police. They were the common enemy.

He rubbed his scratched and irritated eyes. They watered not from lack of sleep nor the biting wind, but rather from the annoying dark brown colored contact lenses which he removed once safely inside. He always had perfect eyesight, but, like his brother, he inherited from their father that particular yellow, almost golden color of the iris. In this country that eye color was very rare and drew attention to his face, and he was not yet ready to be remembered. For that reason he frequently changed the tints of his eyes and tolerated the discomfort from an occasional scratch.

He learned from his father the skills of butchering animals for their meat and the skinning and tanning of their hides. As a young boy, he had spent many hours with his family following the flocks, existing on the animals' sacrifices. The clan had wandered the tribal areas tending their herds, trading the skins and selling the flesh, until the Russians had come.

The brutal torture of the invading infidels with their powerful gunships and large armies had forced his people to fight for their way of life; that's when he learned how to kill and butcher humans. He learned the craft very well and overcame the harsh life. He was one of the fortunate survivors.

After his father and his father's wives were killed, he and his brother traveled the high mountain passes, keeping to the secret paths, and then escaping to the refugee camps. He was skilled at surviving and very devout in his beliefs and was soon selected for training in one of the camps for the mujahedeen. The brothers were eventually able to make their way to London where their paths separated. Appearing as a student, he could travel freely. His friends at the mosque led him into this country and dwelling eight months ago. He spent that time exploring and scouting these hunting grounds. He had learned to wait, not to act on his own impulse, to keep to himself.

16

As he stood and stretched his muscles, he looked about the rooms. They were sparsely furnished, but still contained much more than the caves and the camps of his youth. He had everything he required: a stove with a heavy iron kettle for boiling, a powerful waste compactor for crushing, and a large sink with a very efficient garbage disposal and drain. In front of him, sitting on a heavy metal cabinet, was a plexi-glass box resembling a baby's incubator with a bare fluorescent light hanging above.

By inserting his hands through the gloves in the side of the box, he was able to manipulate the contents without coming into direct contact. He had spent several hours cleaning and preparing the isolated objects inside and now sat back to admire his recently acquired gleaming trophies. His goal was nearing. It was time to prepare for the next kill.

The first animal had been slain many miles away in another state where its desired parts were harvested. The rest of the body was burned and the remains hidden so as not to be found. It would be many months until it was discovered and it could never be traced to his hand.

There were many trophies to be had in this prized American city of Washington and he must collect them quickly before he was identified. Therefore, he must be cunning like the fox and careful to leave some false trails for the police to follow. He would let them become tired from the chase until the trap was ready. That was the purpose of the first random mutilation in the area. There had been no connection to the previous victim miles away, and no relation to the ones that would follow.

The last two specimens, however, had been carefully selected. He'd waited and stalked for one reason: to satisfy his needs. The next animal in this district would be the biggest prize so far, and he was aroused by the thought of a potential challenge. The first three in the district had been so weak and easy.

His current target, like many people in this country, drank alcohol too often and too much. They were creatures of habit and used the same routes to go to the same bars at the same times. After drinking with the other members of their herd all evening, they might become unpredictable, but they were also satiated and less aware of their surroundings. They took more chances than they should, likely making this one simple to harvest.

The time required that he stretch out on his rug in prayer. Then he dressed and put in a different tint of contact lenses. Arming himself with the large knife he had freshened with a stone, just like his father taught him. He was ready to sacrifice another of the unsuspecting infidels.

He traveled some distance on foot through the streets between the tall buildings to the object's customary bar and took up his position to wait in the dark and the cold. He was not long in the shadows before he saw the next animal approaching the watering hole. This one with a heavy coat traveled a bit slower than the others before and was carrying a laptop computer instead of a purse. He noted, *this infidel depends on alcohol so much that he comes to his house of drunkenness before heading home from work.* Also*, these Americans could not go anywhere without their electronic devices.* A cautious thought commanded he not leave that behind after the kill because it could contain some incriminating information.

The hunter with the olive skin, brown eyes and muscular body hid motionless, trancelike, as his prey entered the club. He would wait until his prize stumbled out, follow it into the night and then strike the deadly blow. This carcass, though, would not be left for the police to find.

After several hours, the stalker became aware of a siren. This was a frequent and familiar background noise in the big city, especially after dark, and he took no particular notice of the sound until it came near. Then he saw the ambulance advance down the street and stop directly in front of the door to the bar. The two attendants got out, opened the back of the van and wheeled a stretcher into the establishment. After a short time, they exited with someone now loaded on their cart.

The hunter, still only a shadow, was able to come close enough to see that it was his intended victim. The target's eyes were wide open, and he cried out in pain when the right leg was moved even slightly. Indeed, the leg seemed to be twisted outward at a grotesque angle while being bound to the splint. The patient, along with the heavy coat and computer, was loaded into the vehicle. Even with the severe pain of a broken leg, this one was far better off than he would've been had the predator gotten to him.

The assassin was extremely disappointed, but he must not make the matter worse by being discovered. All he could do for now was to follow the vehicle at a safe distance and determine the destination of the ambulance. The butcher moved easily for about two miles. It was no trouble keeping up with the flashing lights and siren going slowly through the city streets. The van came to a stop outside the emergency room of Good Hope Hospital. Paramedics wheeled the stretcher through the sliding glass doors under the bright lights with the busy cluster of people.

Coldly the hunter turned and slipped back into the night. He would find a way to deal with this unforeseen change; a plan was already coming together in his mind. Resolute, he knew he must have this one. He could wait while the animal was properly prepared for its slaughter. Then, unseen and alone, he would kill and harvest the parts carried inside the body.

Chapter Four

Up on the third floor of Good Hope Hospital in operating room number six, JC was scrubbed in surgery and working hard. He was doing the final adjusting, tweaking the screws and bolts to the tinker-toy-like wires of the external fixation device that he had just placed into the bone with the help of an X -ray image. This allowed him to see and accurately set the broken pieces of the compound fracture of the boy's tibia. The sleeping patient had shattered his lower leg. The pieces stuck out through the skin crusted with all sorts of germs from the clothes and the pavement. This was frequently the result of a motorcycle accident, and JC had to pick out all the blue jean threads and asphalt chunks that he could see and then irrigate the wound with sterile fluid. It was like rinsing milk from a glass until the bacteria were gone; it was nearly impossible to tell when it was clean. Wash out over and over 'til it looked clear, but hit the rest with antibiotics. After that, he could place the metal frame and threaded pins that would hold the bone in place until the shin healed several months later. These gadgets always looked strange sticking out of the leg, but they let the patient get out of the hospital before filing Chapter Eleven and saved many limbs which might have required amputation.

The rich baritone voice of Johnny Cash softly filled the room. The choice of music had been his for this case. He seldom listened outside, but things seemed to go smoother in the OR when country-western music was on the sound system. He thought it was because no one had to concentrate on the common sense lyrics or search for a melody that was obvious, but there seemed to be something about the rhythm that kept things moving along at a calm, steady pace. In spite of the frequent protests, JC noticed that even the younger scrub techs were tapping their feet or humming softly after a few minutes of the music.

It was midnight by now on the cusp of Sunday morning and they had all been working steadily since early afternoon. There was only one more broken femur waiting in the wings that would need surgery tonight and then JC could go home. Even though it was both mentally and physically draining work, these people helping him were tired but tireless. There were easier ways for them to make a living. He'd probably spent more time with this crew than with any other group of people in his recent life, and they were comfortable together in spite of the long hours. Kelly, the circulating nurse, was seated on a stool in front of the computer inputting data while Caroline was scrubbed and sterile and had offered to finish dressing the leg.

When he sighed and sat to write orders, Kelly offered, "Dr. Thomas, you look worn out. How about a cup of strong black coffee and some aspirin?"

"Kelly, you need to realize that this is the twenty-first century, not like the old days. Things have changed. Now, it's a skinny latte and two tamper-proof Tylenol. No ... wait ... with your liver waiting to attack, better make that just one Tylenol."

Before a retort could come, the obnoxious staccato of his pager interrupted the final strains of the man in black.

"Kelly, could you see what they want since you're probably going to be involved anyway?"

"I'm already on the phone to the ER nurse, JC."

As he finished his orders, she hung up and turned to him to speak.

"I'm afraid they've got one you're going to have to go down

and see. Sally says this looks like a broken femur around a total hip. Patient's name is Charles O'Reilly."

The radiology technician was already loading Mr. O'Reilly's X-ray image from the ER on the computer screen as JC walked over to the monitor to get a better look. There was an obvious spiral fracture of the top part of the hollow thigh bone which contained the metal stem of a total hip replacement. This would require surgery at some point, or the man would be miserable and would never be able to walk on this leg again. Although he had seen hundreds of hip replacements, this one was really unusual. The stem that went down inside the middle of the femur was huge in diameter and reached almost all the way down to the knee. It was four or five times bigger than the standard needed in this case. The prosthesis had some resemblance to the type of device that might be put in when cancer had destroyed most of the bone, but that certainly was not the situation here. In fact, the man had an identical component in the other hip.

Caroline looked up and said, "That really looks nasty."

JC agreed. "What do you think guys, about 30 or 40 minutes before we're ready for the next case?"

"Yeah, that sounds about right."

"Well, I better go down to the ER and see what's going on with this one."

"Do you think that's something we'll have to do later tonight?" the anesthetist said from the head of the table.

"No, it's not an emergency and it may take a few days to get him ready. Although we can do without, it's better if we can locate similar replacement parts from the same implant company when we try to fix this. That'll be hard to do. I've never seen anything quite like it. I'll be back up in half an hour, or call me in the ER if you get ready."

JC put on a white coat over his scrubs and took the back stairs down to the emergency room where the waiting area was overflowing as expected on Saturday night. Sick adults and even sicker children spilled out onto the floor.

Some of these people really did need to be here for valid emergencies. Some were here out of convenience. They'd been putting up with their symptoms for several days, were not getting better and couldn't sleep. There were a lot of flu and upper respiratory diseases around this time of year. There was also the usual number of uniformed police officers escorting the chemically impaired who had been brought in off the streets.

Sally was a veteran nurse who had probably taught more practical medicine to more young doctors then any of their professors. This was her Emergency Room. It was not a democracy, and that was a very good thing for the community.

"JC, he's in room seven with a blood alcohol over three times the legal limit," Sally said as he approached the rooms. "Between that and the painkiller, he's in a pretty good mood, but I don't think it's gonna last much longer."

JC entered the room where the nurse was checking the man's IV and introduced himself. He noticed there was no family around.

"Mr. O'Reilly, what in the world went on tonight?"

With slightly slurred speech the man replied, "Doc, everybody calls me Charlie."

"Okay ... most call me JC."

"You see we were out celebrating my birthday and I was tryin' to dance and I guess things got a little carried away. These shoes are old and really slick from the snow and I musta' slipped ... mighta' been some ice on the floor ... anyway ... next thing I know ... I'm lying on the floor with my right leg twisted out and hurting like hell."

"Charlie, your chart says that your birthday was three weeks ago and that you were fifty-four years old. That about right?"

"Yeah, doc, I guess I should tell you the rest of the story if you got time. You see, I'm in estate planning and about six or eight months ago I started having this terrible pain in my groin. I couldn't sleep and really couldn't walk without a cane. That was hurting my business a lot, so I went in to see some other orthopaedic surgeon.

"He took an X-ray and said I had some god-awful kinda arthritis in both my hips. He thought it might have something to do with drinking, but I don't think so—I was just trying to kill the pain. He said it was so far along that I'd probably keep hurting 'til I had my hips replaced.

"Well, I didn't think he knew what he was talking about and I didn't have any health insurance then. All he did was give me some pain pills and they didn't even work very good. Charged me well over a hundred dollars and didn't help at all."

"Sounds like a condition called Osteonecrosis and it can be related to alcohol," JC said. "Taking a lot of cortisone can do that too, and sometimes we just don't know what causes it."

"Well, between you guys and the hospital, I could have bought a new Cadillac for the kind of money it would take to have surgery, so that's when I decided to look into the medical tourism thing.

"Three months ago, I went overseas and had my left hip replaced for less than half the price. They must've done a good job because the pain got a lot better in a few days. I got a vacation at a nice resort and even though I was still weak, I wasn't hurting near as bad. I even picked up some good leads for new clients from the other patients. Three weeks ago I went over again and had my other hip fixed. It was doing so good we decided to go out and celebrate my birthday. Guess I should have picked some better shoes though."

"Charlie, the way you've broken this bone around that stem, I don't see any real good options except for you to have an operation. All of these prostheses are different sizes and shapes and, kind of like Fords and Chevrolets, the parts don't necessarily fit each other. While we can get around that problem by taking the whole thing out, it sometimes helps if we have compatible parts on hand. Where did you say this was done?"

"It was over in the Mediterranean, doc," Charlie yawned. "I've got it all in my laptop there. I guess if you're going to be slicing my leg open, you might as well take my PC and look up the information. I've got names, phone numbers, and even information on the other patients. Some of them were really interested in estate planning."

"Okay, I'll see what I can find out. By the way, did you have any trouble getting through airport security with those artificial hips?"

"No, they give you one of those little cards and wave that

wand thing over you when it shows up on X-ray. Anyway, there were a bunch of us together and I told them where we'd been and we went right on through. They did stop a couple of the gals who had a bottle of perfume that was too big or wasn't in those special little bags. The girls tried to spray enough of it out to get on the plane. It musta worked, but the whole place smelled like a French …a… perfume shop."

"Yeah, there's lots of rules, but I guess we gotta have 'em."

"Doc, I'm sure you saw that I still don't have any medical, but I'll be glad to review your estate for free and try to get you in a good financial position. You know annuities and whole life, that sort of thing."

He was one of those people that you just couldn't help but like, although JC was pretty sure he didn't want Charlie in charge of his estate, at least not right now.

He continued, dozing off between sentences. "Life insurance is really a good investment for the future ... and ... it takes care of your loved ones when you croak ... in case anything ... happens ..."

As Charlie fell asleep JC quietly left and went back to the desk to write some orders. He couldn't help but wonder if that same life insurance company also sold health and accident. Charlie was not the healthiest of patients and was going to need an internist. In addition, he'd have to be watched for withdrawal symptoms, so it would probably be a few days anyway before he could have surgery.

Sally came by again while he was finishing the paperwork.

"Oh, by the way, JC, they called from the OR and your femur got bumped by a C-section for a high risk term pregnancy. They said at least an hour before they could set up your next case, but you can't fuss about that."

"No, way too much at stake for a baby. 'Bout an hour huh? Start about two a.m, be through 'bout three-thirty if we're lucky," he responded. "Sally, you got any aspirin in your purse?"

"JC, you know where that big bottle is in the cabinet over the coffee pot, right where it's always been."

"Think I'll go get two of them."

"Since you're going that way, JC, would you bring me back

a couple?"

It wasn't really a question.

Chapter Five

The hunter felt the cold, wet wind biting his irritated eyes as he retreated from the hospital through the city's pathways. He was confident traveling the dark neighborhoods alone during the nighttime hours. After all, he had spent his life in much more hostile places than this—places where the earth was laden with land mines and the skies held powerful gunships. With his strength and training, armed with the knife, he feared no man. The roving bands in the streets seemed to know; like the rabbits, they fled from the wolf.

Were it not for the attention it could bring, a physical encounter would be a welcome distraction to him now. He was steeled, ready for a contest, but the killing of a single one of these nameless infidels was not part of the plan. The time was coming soon when masses of Americans would again perish and many others would learn to hide in fear and panic.

He was disappointed that the unpredictable American had escaped. The hunter was returning this time without the trophy, but he had enjoyed great success before. His bounty was curing in the box in his basement and needed now to be delivered so that others could prepare the deadly feast. His step quickened; the fires would be starting soon. It was time to offer the prized meats of his slaughter and nothing could interfere with the schedule.

As he approached his flat, he paused at the numbers marking his address and waited while a single truck passed on the street and then turned out of sight in the darkness. The neighborhood was now deserted, asleep from their drugs, no prying eyes to observe. The last tarnished numeral "9" on the door frame was held by a single nail at the top so that it could be rotated, turned just a bit so no one would notice. He precisely swung this digit around a little and pinned the stem in place so that it was no longer pointing straight down. If this were the hand of a clock, the stem now would point to 8:00.

He carefully checked the door and its latch to ensure

nothing had been changed. No intruder had entered. Once safely locked inside, he removed the brown lenses from his scratched and watering eyes. He had three sets of contacts in different tints from light brown to near black. These had been obtained in a city far away where he would not return. One of these lenses had scratched his eyeball and now they all irritated, but he must conceal his true color. He would have to tolerate the nuisance for now. The prizes in his collection were needed.

He began final preparation of the trophies he had acquired. There was one last wash and rinse needed to remove all traces of human contact. With surgical gloves protecting his bounty, the gleaming articles were taken out of the cool glass case one by one, arranged and carefully padded. They must be protected from hands inside the thick boxes. Like ripe fruit, the skin must not be torn. He had been very careful at the harvest to inflect no bruise, to cause no scratch to his prizes.

He placed the packages in an old backpack. Everyone carried these about, so it was the safest, most inconspicuous way to transport through the city. He included a sheet of paper with specific instructions for the placement of the contents. The last part of the instruction told precisely how to dispose of the slip and the backpack and the packing materials. These details were very important at this stage where he had no choice but to trust the others.

While he was busy inside his basement preparing his package, a common yellow taxi that frequently worked in the area passed by on the street outside. The tilt of the last number in the address on the house stood out boldly to the man driving the car. The cab continued slowly down the street, and after making several turns, the "Occupied" light came on. The vehicle and its driver would not be available to hire for the next several hours.

The hunter looked at the telephone in his room and knew it must never be used to call the others. There were no emergency messages recorded. No change in plans. A cell phone could be an even greater risk, and he had never owned one. The leaders had learned from the open trials of those who had gone before. These Americans might listen and could locate the signal. That mistake would not be repeated by his group.

The courier had been summoned, and it was now time to go. The cargo was too important to leave in a hiding place; it must be delivered hand to hand and carefully guarded at each step. He stretched out in prayer as the time required, then replaced his painful lenses, pulled on his coat and cap, and set out with the pack for the selected meeting place miles away from the numerous surveillance cameras which were everywhere in the surrounding region.

After walking many blocks through the nearly deserted streets just before the gray dawn, he boarded the metro for five stops and then walked another mile or so. At precisely eight o'clock, the yellow taxi pulled to a stop near the curb at the location chosen during their last meeting. After being sure of the man at the wheel, he opened the back door.

He had known the driver, Kafeel, since their days together in London, but all he said was, "Nineteenth and U," which was the place of their next meeting. The time for talk and rejoicing would come later. They could not stay together for very long and be observed. The man simply repeated, "Nineteenth and U," as he handed an envelope across the seat. The hunter placed it in his coat and did not bother to look inside. It surely contained twenty-dollar bills for which he might have need. Each note bore a picture, a constant reminder of one of the early beardless rulers of this hated country.

He closed the door and the cab moved away, empty except for a backpack lying on the floor behind the front seat. The driver had one more stop. One more pack to collect before meeting with the last man who would accept the carefully prepared contents. The murderer with the yellow eyes did not need to know anything more. He was the best, but he was just a soldier. Their cause was much too important and too dangerous to trust to only one hunter.

Kafeel received the second package in a similar fashion before he drove across town to a third destination where the taxi stopped and picked up a janitor named Ali. He knew this one was not a hard man like himself and the others, but the custodian had been in place, dormant, waiting just for this time.

After a short ride, the fare who was known at his work as "Al," exited the cab carrying the two packs and walked back to his cheap apartment without drawing attention.

Once alone inside his small room, the man carefully read, memorized, and burned the instructions. He then donned his clean blue uniform, placed his identification badge around his neck, and set out for work just as he had done for the last several years. Ali was the only name he had known from his childhood, but he thought the name, "Al" would draw less attention from the Americans, and indeed that was true. He had patiently managed his position, obeying the laws and doing his job without raising suspicion for many months. In fact, he had recently been given a meaningless merit raise for his good performance. It was not by accident that he closely resembled the laminated picture on his ID badge and the image on his travel documents.

Arriving for his shift, he entered. He was a common sight so he moved easily about the nearly deserted halls of the large building where he was employed. His blue surgical mask, toolbox and pack drew no special attention. This was normal attire for his janitor and handyman jobs. Paper surgical masks were even more common now in his profession, with the flu raging throughout the city. Al was confident. He had been assured that he was a holy warrior, invisible and unsuspected: a man who was about to deliver a significant blow to the infidels.

The custodian moved about the rooms, carefully installing the contents of the pack as he had been instructed in the note, with just a screwdriver and a small pocketknife. He was unnoticed until one of his crew walked in on him while he was placing the last of the items. She was one of the shameless women who did not know her place. She held her head high and looked directly at his face. Her uniform barely covered her knees when walking. This one would need to be beaten often by her husband, but her body could bear many sons.

"Hey, Al, whatcha doing?"

The mask hid his surprise.

"I'm doing a final check in here. You go clean that room across the hall."

He had no time to bother with this girl now. She painted her face and kept the hair removed from her legs. He had noticed that about her before. The woman turned and left without a second thought. She had seen nothing.

Al finished the final steps of preparation. The seeds had been planted in several places now, exactly as instructed by the burned paper. It had taken several hours, but now he felt satisfied with his work. The weapons were ready, and the triggers would soon be pulled. Many American deaths would follow.

His task completed, he walked outside for nearly a mile and disposed of the old packs in one of the many dumpsters some distance away. The man who called himself Al started a winding path back to his job, but stopped and sat down on a bench to rest and watch. It was there that he ate his supper before returning to the nearby building to stand guard and perform some of his normal duties for the evening's event. He chose to eat in a small park surrounded by concrete panels. On these walls were chiseled the names of many American Peace Officers who had been killed while pursuing the lawless. He was pleased to know that because of him, they would soon need to add many more panels.

As with many workers who routinely perform maintenance and cleaning around metal objects with sharp tools, he was completely unaware of the new deep scratch he had received on the back of his hand. Even while eating his sandwich, he barely took notice of the few drops of dried blood that had accumulated there.

Chapter Six

Slicing through the deepest layers of sleep came the cacophonous sound of the Claxton. Honk ... Honk ... Warning ... the security threat to the entire nation has just risen to the highest possible level ... Honk ... Honk ... total destruction is imminent in 10 ... 9 ... 8 ... 7....6... No, no ... wait ... it was much worse.

JC managed to get one eye half open after a struggle. He could just make out the glaring tone of the bedside alarm clock honking loudly from the red stick figures defiantly proclaiming "5:00 am"

It couldn't possibly be right. His head had just touched the pillow. The electricity must have failed again from an ice storm. There it was, though ... now "5:01." Guided by his one functioning eye, JC was able to reach out and tenderly caress the cool, bare shoulder of the alluring snooze bar. It failed to respond, unmoved, incapable of emotion until he found the exact spot and applied more force, then finally ... quiet. In an instant, the blaring began, again. The red sticks demanded, "5:08 ... And this time I mean it!" Some teenager's mother who was an ex-coach or a gym teacher must have programmed the clock.

He was so very, very tired, but it was Monday morning and the good news was that he'd survived another forty-eight straight hours of emergency room call with only five hours of sleep. JC spent almost all day Sunday and the better part of the night between the ER and the operating room. He got home at two. He would be responsible for emergencies every fifth weeknight in addition to the normal work load, but he would not have to cover Saturday-Sunday again for a whole month.

JC considered the siren song of the snooze bar again, but instead, dragged himself out of bed and made it all the way down the hall, past the bathroom, and into the kitchen. Once there, he passed the first real test of the week when he found the "Start" button on the espresso machine.

While the coffee brewed, he stumbled back to the bathroom and lathered cream on his face. He always shaved meticulously. It probably didn't look too good when surgeons showed up with multiple little patches of bloody toilet paper on their faces. The coffee was ready and the welcomed smell was starting to work its magic.

By the time he had showered and dressed in his usual slacks, open collar shirt and sweater vest, he was beginning to look forward to the day though he was still not quite there yet. He carefully placed new batteries in his pager as a peace offering to keep it in a good mood for the week.

JC locked all the doors, set the security alarm and lowered the thermostat. He then headed out to his car, which was parked on the short driveway beside the house. *Okay.* he promised himself again. This weekend he would clean out the garage and make room for the vehicle. No excuses.

Though the snow had stopped, it was still overcast, and there were small patches of ice on the pavement. He drove around the beltway in traffic that was a bit lighter than the usual Monday morning and exited to approach his office through the city streets. He detoured through the donut place and picked up two dozen assorted for the office staff. Well, he might have one of the jelly-filled for breakfast.

As was often the case, he was the first of the office people to arrive. He liked a little quiet time to collect and catch up before the hectic Monday started. JC gathered the three newspapers which were always stacked outside the front door before he arrived, and he wondered what cruel time the delivery man must get up to start his route so dutifully each day.

With his second cup of coffee in hand, he prioritized the sections of the paper for scanning. Staying up to date was difficult but necessary in order to run a small business and be able to communicate with his patients.

First in importance was the sports page. The home team had hit a three point shot at the buzzer last night to move within a half game of first place. He couldn't remember them ever being at the top this late in the season. They would be playing here this weekend against the first place team. If they won, next stop playoffs!

He had almost forgotten, he'd been so busy. One of his partners, who served as the orthopaedic consultant for the basketball team, had offered him two tickets for the upcoming game. Who he would invite to go with him required some thought. Nobody came immediately to mind. The only candidates right now were either nurses he worked with or sister-in-laws of doctors he knew. Neither was a good choice for the long run.

Next in importance in the paper came the local news where it was reported that the area hospitals were overflowing with respiratory disease from colds and flu in the elderly and the immune-compromised. He could personally verify that story judging by the large ER crowds he had witnessed over the weekend.

Another local article said that a suspected serial killer had brutally murdered and then horribly mutilated three women in the metro area. The investigations were ongoing, but the police weren't giving out any other details and no arrests had been made. JC had always been a voracious reader; that's what got him through school. The problem now was, there was just so much out there to be read. He had to scan.

In most medical and scientific articles, the authors tried to eliminate their bias. If the math was done properly, there was usually some truth gained by reading the title and the brief abstract. He'd found that the newspapers, however, required a different approach: skip the first one or two paragraphs of the writer's opinion and some facts might be found buried in the body of the story.

The front sections of the paper contained the national and international news. The politicians continued to plagiarize Charles Dickens. To the party in power it was the best of times, while the party out of power maintained that it was the worst of times. Both yearned for a return to the good old days. To JC, it depended on the point of view. Yes, gas was cheaper back then, but half of the patients who broke their hip never left the hospital. The air was cleaner, but most heart attack victims didn't make it to the hospital, and the ones that did usually died shortly thereafter.

Continuing to read, he was informed that recent peace talks had been suspended but would resume at a later date. The tax rate was too high/low and needed to be changed. A prominent elected official was suspected of something, and a bipartisan committee needed to be formed. JC put the paper down, letting all of the new knowledge soak in. It was time to get to work.

He now opened Charlie's laptop. Having once lost a ton of important data, JC had learned. First thing he did when he got the computer was to copy the necessary files from Charlie's computer and leave that disc in the trunk of the car; his usual secure storage bin. Now, he reviewed the folders on the desktop that were pertinent to his patient's recent experience. He noted that the man was very organized and that there was a lot of information about the medical tour. There was a second file that contained names, addresses and phone numbers of what he assumed were traveling companions on the man's two trips, and also potential future clients.

It could be a big help if he identify the brand and style of the device in Charlie's hip before surgery. He dialed the 800 number listed in the computer for Imperial Medical Tours. After several rings, however, a pleasant female voice from the phone company informed him that this was no longer a working number and there was no forwarding.

He then went to the webpage for Imperial. It was a very well done site headlined by the fact that surgical procedures performed overseas were significantly cheaper than those done in this country and were followed by a fabulous vacation in an exotic resort! It went on to explain that this agency specialized in cosmetic surgery, dental implants and total joint replacement.

There were numerous glowing testimonials and pictures, but due to medical privacy concerns, these patients' names could not be made available—a part of the service you would come to appreciate! He also saw that all of the prostheses used in hips and knees were FDA-approved. This struck him as a bit odd. They were indeed a powerful bunch, but JC hadn't realized their administrative authority extended that far outside the United States. Unfortunately, the website was temporarily not responding to further inquiries.

In Charlie's file was a phone number of the overseas hospital. JC didn't recognize the country's numerical prefix. He had been stationed at the large airbase in Turkey several years ago. During that time he had become well-versed in International calling around the Mediterranean in order to communicate with various healthcare professionals at other military installations. JC had served his time in the military in order to help receive his education. Though he greatly respected the institution and the people he met there he knew this wasn't a life intended for him. Looking at the number, again, he speculated this number might be in an area of the eastern Mediterranean that had a reputable state run medical system with clean, up to date hospitals.

While waiting for the call to be completed, he reflected on the week of R and R he'd enjoyed while on active duty attached to the base. He had toured the Mediterranean resorts and had been impressed with the beautiful scenery, the warm climate, and the friendly, outgoing people. He could almost taste the fresh seafood flavored by the local herbs and absent the MSG. He really should go back there with someone special sometime, but there hadn't been someone special for some time now.

JC also recalled that the area continued to be a playground for the rich and the filthy rich, and like any large playground, there was a giant sandbox. And like any sandbox, if you sat in it too long, you would get grit in your bathing suit and parasites in places you couldn't scratch.

After several minutes he was connected to the hospital administrator who spoke fluent English.

"Why yes, Dr. Thomas, I remember Imperial. They were here two weeks ago for the third time."

"You see," the man continued, "from time to time the state run medical system fills its quota of patients that are allowed to have surgery and still stay within the budget. Instead of closing, we lease the hospital to various reputable groups."

The renters apparently paid a fee directly to the administrator who then paid the nurses. The highly trained anesthesia and staff were all utilized to insure that the patients had the very best of care.

"This is all perfectly acceptable practice," the man said, "and the nurses appreciate the extra income."

No, he didn't know anything about the implants except he was told they were FDA-approved. They were always brought in by the Imperial people themselves. Perhaps the chief surgery nurse could help him. While waiting for her to come on the line, the administrator graciously invited JC to visit and perhaps perform some surgery in his facility. After a short pause, the nurse came on the line. Her English was not quite as good, but passable to JC's ear. Of course she remembered. That particular group had been there on three different occasions in the last few months. The orthopaedic surgeon, she thought might have been from Pakistan. He had those golden-yellow eyes, and was a well-trained product of the British system. He was not an especially outgoing person. He was rather stern, actually, and she really didn't know much about him. He seemed to look down on the women of her staff. They thought he was arrogant and didn't like to work with him, but they needed the money, so they tolerated the situation.

She thought the dentist was Saudi and the plastic surgeon was American. She complimented their work, but she hadn't seen

34

any of them for the last two weeks. Yes, the group did bring in their own implants for both the augmentation Mammoplasties and the Orthopaedic procedures, but the nurse didn't know what brand they might have been. Some of her surgery techs had commented that the hip implants were really large and heavy, a bit unusual looking. The people from Imperial were the only ones allowed to handle them. She assumed that they were much cheaper than those expensive devices used in the United States and suspected that was one way to save on costs.

The breast implants looked like those used in other parts of the world, although again, her techs were not allowed to handle these. That was a bit of a sticking point. Her techs were as good as anywhere else, even though they didn't do that kind of surgery under the state-run system. Her hospital, of course, could not be responsible for the devices. She continued by saying that after a few days of acute recovery in the hospital, the patients were taken to a resort to further recuperate. She was not aware of any significant complications. Imperial looked like they did good work, but of course, she had no long-term follow-up information.

Oh, she had almost forgotten. After they packed up and left last time, she had discovered that four of anesthesia's large gas-containing cylinders were missing: two of the big green colored ones for oxygen and two of nitrous oxide. The chief nurse thought it was just a mistake, but she hadn't been able to get through on Imperial's e-mail. If he was able to get in contact with them, might he let her know.

Before leaving the line she remarked that her hospital was in a very secure area and she hoped that Dr. Thomas would visit and perhaps perform some surgery while he was there. He appreciated the invitation. He told her how much he missed the beautiful scenery of the region but how the demands of his current work schedule did not permit such an itinerary. Then he hung up the phone.

Strike one.

JC then called Max, the sales representative of the company currently under contract to supply prostheses to his hospital. It was Max's job to be informed about his own company's implants. Of course, like any good rep, he was also quite familiar with the competition's products. When he arrived, they reviewed the x-ray images of Charlie's hip on the computer monitor.

"I've never seen anything like that," JC said. "Got any ideas?"

"No," Max responded. "I've never seen anything that big used for elective surgery. It kinda' looks like those special devices used by cancer surgeons when a large portion of the femur bone has been eaten away and has to be substituted with metal."

"Yeah, but that's not the case here," JC continued. "In fact, he's got another one just like it on the opposite side and no history of cancer. I don't see any evidence of bone cement or rough coating to ever lock the bone into the metal. Looks like they just dropped that gigantic stem down in there and it's doomed to get loose and fail."

"Maybe it's some experimental device that's being trialed in Europe or Asia?"

"Could be, I guess," JC said, "but I sure don't see any advantages. I can't imagine this would last comfortably for over six months to a year before it began to destroy the underlying bone and really start hurting. If there's any good news, the socket side looks pretty conventional and we may get by without having to re-do it."

Charlie was stable and would be ready for the operating room tomorrow. It would be a rather complicated case, and since there were no compatible parts in the Washington area, JC would need Max to have available the special equipment necessary. JC would have to remove all the existing hardware except maybe the socket side of the hip, set the broken bone, and then replace the failed stem with a whole new expensive revision component. The fact that Max didn't have any idea about the implement currently within Charlie's leg peaked JC's interest.

Strike two.

The morning clinic was unusually busy with the extra patients who'd been hurt over the weekend. They needed to be seen to discuss surgery options, refill their pain meds, have work excuses written. There was no way to keep on schedule. By twelve-thirty he was able to run out to of the front of the office, but by then all the donuts had gone missing. Skipping lunch, JC made it just in time for the afternoon's scheduled surgeries. They were rather routine cases that went smoothly, and, luckily, caffeine and adrenaline still worked.

Walking to his car, JC noticed that the winter sky had cleared and the stars were as bright as luminal on blood splatter. Once out of the metro area, JC stopped by for a pepperoni and mushroom pizza to go, fought the traffic, and locked himself in his house where he ate almost the whole thing. He barely made it through the news before he fell asleep on the couch and later crawled to his bed for seven full hours of sleep.

Chapter Seven

The sound of the alarm was not quite as violent as it had been the day before, but it still was a shock to JC's auditory system. The snooze bar had been worth a single touch this morning, more like a peck on the cheek, but it was becoming obvious to both that they wouldn't be spending a lot of time together. The irritating honking noise just couldn't be shut out for very long. JC had read that some people were protesting the use of a particular brand of clock as violations of the Geneva Convention against enemy combatants. This particular Tuesday, he was sympathetic to their cause. It must be this brand.

The muscles in his body were stiff and tight from the weekend, and he tried to stretch just like he told his patients all the time. It did help enough that he became aware of the dull headache from sleeping too long at one time, trying to catch up. JC was on call for his group, again, today. The result of some foolish trade he'd made for some good reason long ago.

Taking advanced call was like accruing air miles--someday it would really pay off. He was way up in the plus column. Thinking about this, he was beginning to feel a bit better. By the time he'd taken the universal antidotes of coffee and a warm shower, he was starting to think about the challenge of Charlie's revision surgery posted for 7:30 a.m. After his usual morning routine, he walked out to the drive and started the cold car while renewing his vows to clean out the garage this weekend. Saturday was still a long way off.

Once the defroster cleared the Rorschach blot test of ice crystals from his windshield and he backed out into the street. It was a forty-five-minute commute to the hospital. Nobody was paying proper attention. *Please, people, be careful,* he thought, *I'm on call today.* It looked like most of the drivers were on their cell phones conducting business with all the other drivers through their ear pieces. Someone was telling every other car to swerve into the lane and cut each other off until they approached downtown and the traffic thickened near his exit. Then the word went out for every vehicle in front of him to stop and idle, and for every large truck behind him to drive right on in to his backseat.

He survived the trip, again, by avoiding the confused out-of-towners caught in the traffic circles and the stop and go double-decker tour buses. By the time he arrived at the hospital, the gate was broken again and every place in the doctors' lot was taken, but on his third trip around, one of his colleagues waved him in as he was leaving. It would be good to get into a nice quiet, relaxing operating room.

Morning rounds went well. He gradually discharged the orthopaedic patients who had accumulated from the weekend. As commonly happens during flu season, all the hospitals were strapped for beds, and those who were stable would probably have less risk of infection if they continued their rehab elsewhere. Even some who lived alone could get by with visiting nurses and were ready for the privacy of their own homes.

After rounds, JC stopped in the pre-op holding room to check Charlie's most recent lab work and to answer any last minute questions. Anesthesia had just finished their discussion, and Charlie was in the process of turning the conversation toward the more important subject of long term estate planning when JC walked in.

"Good morning, Mr. O'Reilly, how are you doing? Any questions come up about the surgery I explained last night?"

With a grin from beneath the tilted bouffant paper hat, Charlie replied, "Come on, doc, give me a break."

JC had heard every variation on this common orthopaedic theme a thousand times, but still, when Charlie said it, he couldn't help but smile.

"By the way, anybody waiting outside for you?"

"Yeah, quite a few. I gave the girl a list that it's okay to talk to after you get finished."

The sedative was starting to work. Charlie dozed off as he was wheeled into the operating room. Completely asleep the traction on his leg was removed before he was lifted onto the OR bed. A tube was placed in his trachea by the anesthesiologist to ensure his airway would stay open throughout the long case. JC helped to turn and position him with his right side up where he'd written "JCT" on the incision site and he checked to be sure that any prominent areas were well padded to prevent pressure sores.

While the circulating nurse prepped the skin, JC washed his hands with the bactericidal soap. The surgical techs had been in the room for at least half an hour arranging the tons of equipment they would need, and now they helped him dress in the familiar sterile space suit, gown and two pair of gloves like they had on. The HEPA filters behind the vents in the wall took almost all the germs out of the room, and the cleanest air in Washington bathed the patient, the tools and supplies.

This type of filter had been used for years in special operating rooms to decrease the number of bacteria present. They were now commonly found in the heating and cooling ducts of many buildings. They could trap even the smallest of particles. It could get quite stuffy in the surgical hood, especially when he started to exert energy, but once he became accustomed to the noise of a fan circulating air inside the helmet, this was a rather enviable environment: no germs, no pollens, no telephone and, most importantly, no beeper.

There is a certain tension in an OR, even among the practiced. Once everyone's dressed and huddled around a sleeping patient that a surgeon is about to make bleed while working on a long and difficult procedure. In this case, JC's assistants happened to all be female, and as they crowded intimately together, he remarked, "This is like me being trapped alone in a phone booth with three pretty women ... my junior high fantasy come true."

Caroline, not a fan of country music, managed a different reply every time she heard this line.

"Well, that's if you don't count Waylon and Willie and the

Boys in here with us."

Rachel, who'd been there for less than a year, asked, "Dr. Thomas, what's a phone booth, anyway?"

"Rachel, you'll have to ask your mother when you get home tonight. In the meantime, pass me that knife ... please."

He opened the previous incision with the scalpel and dissected through the flesh. The original surgery appeared to have been a well-done, classic surgical approach between the layers of muscle around the hip. The tissue was a bit distorted from the previous operation and the subsequent fractured bone, but with the assistants' help, he was able to expose the artificial ball and socket without too much difficulty.

After he located the hip, he observed that the sphere that had been placed on the metal stem looked fairly normal. These modular balls, often a shiny alloy of chrome, came in different sizes and fit down on the stem much like the top locks straight down on a fountain pen. It was removed by simply pulling or tapping it off. Once that was done, it was easy to take out the entire twelve inch long cylinder of metal that had been dropped down in the hollow of the femur like a dowel.

He briefly examined this stem and noticed that the material had a dull silver appearance and seemed to be more fragile and less refined than most modern day prostheses. The outside was smooth and there was no way it could have ever become fixed to the bone.

"That's the biggest stem I've ever seen. It must weigh over ten pounds," Max said. He had come in to watch and stood against the far wall. "Yeah, I believe you now hold the American record. We should take a picture with you holding that monster up. The biggest ones we make are only about four pounds. Nobody's gonna' believe this."

"That device looks like it could'a been made in a muffler shop or in somebody's garage. It was doomed to fail at some point," JC said. "Unfortunately, I can see a lot of problems coming from his other hip not too far down the road." He turned to the circulating nurse and asked, "Kelly, would you put on some gloves and take that thing from Caroline? Be careful it's heavy and very slick, looks like it'd shatter if you dropped it, but then that wouldn't be a great loss."

"I've got it. Now, what do you want me to do with it?"

"If you don't mind, rinse it off and soak it in Cidex to kill any germs from overseas. My partner has an infected one that was put in over in India that he's dealing with already. It's becoming more and more of a problem for us here."

Kelly, ever the optimist, said, "I hope we don't run out of germ killer trying to sterilize that thing."

"After we get through today, I'd like to take that over to the office to look at some more, but not right now, we'd better get moving," JC said.

The rest of the case went rather smoothly. He set the fractured femur, which was broken much like the spiral produced when a can of refrigerated biscuits is twisted open. Then, he wrapped wire cable around it at several different places. Finally once the tube of bone had been restored, he placed an expensive new titanium stem that Max had brought in and it fit tightly inside the hollow cavity. This one had a rough, porous coating to allow the body to grow bone into the pores and could withstand the tremendous forces that would be placed on it for the next thirty or more years.

Ashley was called to come in and take an x-ray, which always took more operating time, but saved some unpleasant surprises later. The image looked good and the sponges which had been used to soak up the blood in the big wound were all accounted for, so JC put in a plastic drain tube and sewed the incision back together in multiple layers. The raw bone would continue to ooze for a few days--the first step toward healing, but so far the blood loss was less than a unit.

After the dressings were applied, post-op orders were written and the patient was safely taken to recovery, JC went out to the small, confidential waiting room. Charlie had no immediate family present, but he had many acquaintances, friends, and possibly some clients concerned about their estates.

Having been given permission beforehand, JC informed the group that the surgery had gone well. The removed prosthesis was apparently a different type of device than that used in this country; he would like to take it to his office that afternoon for further study. He expected Mr. O'Reilly would need at least another three to four days in the hospital. Assuming no complications, JC was optimistic that Charlie would have a comfortable, stable hip on that side for a number of years. The patient would have to use crutches for at least six weeks, but all of his friends said they would be glad to pitch in and help.

A stout man with an olive complexion and brown eyes, obviously a caring relative or good friend to some other patient having surgery that day, blended in with the masses in the large, crowded outer waiting room. He didn't go into the small private area with the doctor. He was not on the list, but he did manage to mingle, unnoticed, near Charlie's talkative friends afterwards.

It was easy for this man to learn that a Dr. John C. Thomas had successfully performed the redo hip surgery and that the doctor was planning to take the removed device to his office later that day for further study. The man was also pleased to discover that Charlie had tolerated the operation very well and would probably be discharged to his home after another three to four days in a weakened condition.

The unidentified visitor left the hospital shortly thereafter without stopping in the gift shop to order flowers. They would be needed by others later. He was a very patient man, and he had a lot of practice. He could wait.

Chapter Eight

JC had one more case before he changed into his street clothes and collected the sterile prosthesis that Kelly had put in a plastic bag for him to take. He placed Charlie's removed hip device in the trunk of his car for safe keeping beside several computer disks that he had accumulated, and then hurried to his office for an afternoon of appointments.

Once the office visits were completed, he returned to the hospital in the twilight to check on his post-op patients. Had he forgotten to eat again? He must have because a dull headache was starting to form. He probably needed more coffee with extra sugar.

With a fresh hot cup in hand, he went to the nurse's station and reviewed the charts. Next, he went in to see Charlie who awakened enough to wiggle his toes up and down before falling back to sleep. The vital signs were stable, and his blood count was still good. He was comfortable with no evidence of complication and had a steady stream of approved visitors. Of course, the IV containing morphine was a considerable help.

JC returned to the nurse's station to carefully record the brief exam of his patient in the progress notes. Should JC die from overwork during the night, Charlie would have excellent continuity of care once his grieving partners referred to these notes.

One of the floor nurses was busy charting, and another was preparing to give medication. Dr. Mason Short, an excellent internist, was sitting at the desk looking at a monitor. JC thought he'd seen him there when he first came on the floor some time ago. Must be a tough case, he thought.

"Oh. Hi there, JC. Got a minute?" he said with his head tilted down.

"Sure, Mason. What's up?"

"You remember my wife, Linda, from the hospital Christmas party?"

"Yeah, I was wondering how you got so lucky to find her," JC said. "Why, is she alright?"

"Oh Linda is fine, thanks," Dr. Short responded, and without pause he continued, "we were talking last night and she reminded me that you came to that party back in December all alone, and her sister from Chicago just got divorced and is going to be in town this weekend. She thought it would be fun if we all went out to dinner Saturday night at a nice restaurant, what do you say?"

"Oh, well I'm sorry," JC said as his beeper began to chirp. "I've already made plans for the basketball game this weekend."

For once, his beeper sounded like the bugle call of the Calvary coming to the rescue.

"Excuse me. It's the ER. I better get it."

When he reached for the phone, he noticed the nurses' ears return to their normal positions. JC would have to remember to thank the ER for calling. He smiled. The ER probably was never thanked for calling.

He was sure Dr. Short's sister-in-law was nice, and Linda meant well, but he'd spent several awkward evenings with good friend's sisters. Besides, he was not running an escort service here. There was already too much competition in the D.C. area.

There were two more broken arms to tend to in the ER before he retreated home. Hopefully this would be a night when people went to bed early and safely, and he would not have to come out in the winter weather.

JC was too tired to cook and he was on call anyway, so he stopped by again for pizza, pepperoni and mushroom. He parked in the drive and let himself in to the dark, quiet house and punched in the security alarm code. After the microwave had done its magical re-warming, he glanced through the mail. Most of the important stuff went to the office anyway. JC propped his feet up with the gourmet delicacy on the thick cardboard serving dish and watched the 10 o'clock news, trying to relax.

On the screen, Chief Investigator Murray Lane informed him that the first Jane Doe had been identified, confirmed by fingerprints and dental records. She had been a single mother of two minor children visiting from out of the area. Her former husband and coworkers had been interviewed and were no longer under suspicion. The children were being cared for by their grandmother.

The well-liked young woman had been working and attending school. She had no criminal record and toxicology screening was negative for drug use. If anyone had helpful information would they please call the number on the screen.

Forensics could so far neither confirm nor deny that there were similarities to the other two victims in the manner of death, and there was absolutely no evidence that she had ever known the other two women nor had any connections to them. The investigation was still in the early stages. A lot of people were working around the clock on solving these cases, and the Chief would accept no questions at this time. He would inform the public as soon as any new developments occurred. Again, citizens in the area were advised to take all reasonable precautions.

The news anchor interpreted what the Chief had just said. She proclaimed, "There was a deranged serial killer on the loose who could strike again at any minute. There was no reason to panic. Handgun sales had tripled this week. Use common sense and stay in groups when traveling at night. Lock all the doors and windows in your home. Be sure to check every single one of your closets. Look under the bed before falling asleep, and for God's sake, stay tuned to this channel. It may very well save your life!"

One beer; one new and used car sales; and one discount reclining leather chair commercial later, and then, finally, the sports news came on. It had been confirmed that the starting point guard had slightly sprained his ankle yesterday in practice. He was recovering (under the expert care of JC's partner, no doubt). He was able to practice at 83%. It was expected that he would be 100% for the game on Saturday, which would determine the conference lead. JC had forgotten again that he had been promised tickets for the game, and he would need to put some thought into who he should ask to go with him. He'd think about it later; he was much too tired now.

As he turned the TV off and got into bed, JC carefully tucked in his electronic pager and placed it on the nightstand next to the phone and the alarm clock. He almost said "goodnight" to his intimate friend, the hospital beeper, but was asleep before his head touched the pillow. The pager turned on him and retaliated for the unintended slight in the worst possible way when it began to chirp loudly at 2:37 am. It was the ER.

In his mind there were two extremes of ER nurse calls in the middle of the night. One that insisted upon giving the entire past history, family history, financial and social history, followed by the physical examination and the x-ray findings, and let him drift back to sleep before asking what to do. And then there was Sally.

"Dr. Thomas, we need you to come in right away. I'll track down the ER doctor to give you the details while you're in your car."

Sally had run the ER night shift for years, but must have been a first grade teacher in a previous life. There was no question that she was always right. She'd heard every excuse, and her instructions needed to be followed. Her voice would not allow anyone to go back to sleep.

In three minutes he'd thrown on his clothes, run to the car, and was talking to the crusty ER doctor while rushing to the hospital. He was informed that a young man returning home on his motorcycle, probably after a late night prayer meeting, tried to pass the car in front of him which was only going sixty-five miles an hour. On a patch of ice, he spun out and struck a concrete barrier that was only going zero miles an hour.

Luckily, the man was wearing a helmet and had no life threatening injuries. Unfortunately, he sustained a dislocation of his ankle and the pressure cut off the circulation to the foot. The ER doctor had tried to reduce this upon arrival but was not successful. JC would need to get this back in place in short order or the young man would lose his foot.

Driving carefully on the icy road, he still arrived at the hospital in 17 minutes. After a quick glance at the x-ray, he saw the cold, pulseless foot. The man had been medicated through the IV and was heavily sedated. There was no family and no time to wait for informed consent. JC knew exactly what to do.

He elicited the help of a muscular ER attendant, and by quickly applying significant force in the correct direction he was able to feel and hear the satisfying "thunk" of a joint being restored to its normal position. The pulse in the foot returned almost immediately, and the toes began to resume their normal pink color. A splint was placed to maintain the reduction and the young man was admitted to the hospital. He would need to have a plate and screws applied to the broken bones when his condition was more stable, but that part was not considered to be an emergency. He was comfortable with no immediate risk to the foot, and it would be safer to wait until his stomach was empty of liquid refreshment.

After finishing the paperwork, JC had three lousy options. One, he could return home and sleep for an hour, which usually put him in a worse mood. Two, he could return home and call in sick tomorrow with the flu. After all, half the people around had it. He did have a headache, but people were counting on him, sick or not. Three, he could go to his nearby office where there were a shower, a razor, and a change of clothes, and maybe get two hours of sleep if nothing else came up.

JC got in his car and drove the six blocks to his office. As he pulled up to the front of the building, he noticed that it was almost five o'clock, and there were no newspapers in front of the door, yet. He went out into the freezing darkness, and when he reached the lighted entry, a member of the late-night cleaning crew was just leaving with a backpack and a toolbox. The man seemed startled and glanced up only briefly without speaking. His eyes were the bright yellow color of Staphylococcus Aureus, making the face unforgettable.

The man then disappeared into the night on foot as JC watched his retreat. A minute later, the newspaper delivery van pulled up to the curb, and a large man with an olive complexion, a full beard, and a load of papers walked up.

"Hello there. I'm John Thomas. I work here."

"My name is Muhammad, but most people call me Mo."

"First time I've ever beaten you here," JC said. "What time do you hav'ta get up anyway?"

"Actually, I am employed elsewhere during the night, and I come directly to this position from a second job. It is good to meet you, but I must go to stay on schedule."

"Well, thanks Mo. Here, I'll take those in."

JC pushed open the door to the suite of offices that he shared with his four partners. Strange, he thought, the housekeeper had forgotten to lock up. As soon as the lights came on, the chaos was obvious. Someone had ransacked the place. They left files and cabinets ajar. The cash drawer hung open and empty. Office instruments and old orthopaedic implants littered the floor. JC surveyed the huge mess.

He stopped himself before going any farther. Having dealt with desperate, unpredictable druggies frequently in the ER, he could not be sure that they were all gone. He ran back out looking for the housekeeper, who was nowhere in sight, before he considered what he would do if he did find the man. The smartest thing would be to wait outside and call the police from there. He retreated a few more steps and reached for his cell. Over the last six or seven months, JC had become used to being alone with no one to talk to, but it was strangely comforting now to hear from someone who cared.

"911. What is your emergency?"

Chapter Nine

Most residents of Washington had learned to close their ears to the noise of a distant siren or else they never got any sleep. The sound came too often and always with a built in reason to not listen. It was probably just another drug-related tragedy in the projects, or maybe it was one of the police escorts for a "Look at Me" visiting Somebody from Somewhere who came to town twice a day. It could be the President was just taking his family across town for breakfast in one of those black SUV's they all seemed to like so much.

When JC heard the whooping cough sound it always reminded him of a baby with respiratory distress struggling to breath. It meant someone else was in trouble and he could help; he was in control. Not this time. Now, he was waiting for someone else to take charge and help him. It was a very strange, uncomfortable feeling. The doctor had become the patient, and as any nurse could attest, they weren't very good at it.

JC had started the morning grumpy then passed through surprise and anger but was now back to frustration. He'd just let the thief walk right on by. Then he considered, *what would he have done if he'd caught up with him? Worse still, what if he'd come upon that cold looking creature inside his office?* He waited outside in the cold darkness with uncertainty and apprehension while he pondered these possibilities. It wasn't long before the familiar white car with "POLICE" boldly written on its side screeched to a halt at the curb. He had reported a burglary in progress and the two uniformed patrolman sprang out of the vehicle with their guns drawn. A dog's massive head filled the space in the back window. Barking and growling he looked like he hadn't had a taste of bad guy all week and was ravenously eyeing JC's throat. Maybe just a little bite of something in his stomach would tide him over.

JC was careful to keep his hands in sight. He'd read about cases of mistaken identity, and he probably did look a little suspicious. Reddened eyes and stubble of whiskers on his face, blood stains and white plaster casting material spotting the green scrub pants under his lab coat, but he could explain, honestly. He'd been up most of the night working in the Emergency Room.

The officers must have known his relief, probably seen this a thousand times, as they approached where he was standing.

"Glad to see you guys. I'm Dr. Thomas. I'm the one who called in," JC stated as he handed them his ID.

"What's going on?" One of the officers inquired as he returned the card to him.

"I just finished a case in the ER and don't usually come by this early. The door to my office was unlocked so 1 went on in and hit the lights. The place had been trashed. Guess they're looking for drugs."

"You think they're still in there?"

"I don't think so. There was a creepy looking guy leaving as I got here ... thought it'd be better to wait back out here 'til you came."

"Good idea. Some of these people are pretty cranked. Why don't you stay here and we'll check it out."

The two men entered the building, watching each other's back with flashlights and weapons in hand, while JC stood by the front door trying to avoid eye contact with Professor Pavlov's dog who was drooling in the backseat. After a few minutes, the men returned and holstered their side arms. One of them began a conversation with his shoulder that included a lot of the 10-something ... crackle ... crackle ... words, while the dog replaced his tongue and tried to hide his disappointment 'til the next bell rang.

The other officer turned to JC and said, "You're right, it's a real mess, and there's nobody left inside. Let's wait here a minute. One of the big bosses of the robbery division was on the way into work passing nearby and should be showing up pretty soon. You're lucky, they're spread so thin in burglary usually they have to send one of the newbies."

A minute or two later, a black Crown Victoria with that exempt license plate, sped up to the curb and stopped. It looked like any other standard unmarked police car until the door opened and an officer in civilian clothes got out. No trench coat, no cigar, just shoulder length brown hair and a dark business suit. She walked straight up to the three waiting men. With a clipboard in one hand, and Coke can in the other, she looked JC in the eye and said, "Hello, Dr. Thomas, I'm Lt. Lauren Long."

Without waiting for a reply, she turned to one of the patrolmen.

"Sgt. Davis, what have you found so far?"

"Looks like a routine break-in. Forced the door lock, a little more sophisticated jumping off the alarm than usual, and then they tore up everything inside the office."

"Do you keep drugs or much cash on hand?" she asked JC.

"No, we don't keep any narcotics or pain medicines, but there are some steroids and Xylocaine. There shouldn't be over $100, if that much. If there were any cash payments, the girls take them to the bank every night."

"Good idea, but you do keep syringes and needles?"

"Yes, we inject some joints with Cortisone and use some local deadening medicine for minor procedures."

"Well, they were most likely after drugs, but they'll take anything nowadays. Probably had nothing to do with your personnel, but we will need a list of the people that worked here for the last six months and the name of your cleaning service. Any business contacts or patients you can think of that might have a reason to break in?"

"Nobody comes to mind, but there're always a few disgruntled customers," JC said. "But when I came up about five this morning, there was this guy I thought was the housekeeper who really looked suspicious. He brushed past me in a hurry to get out and didn't say a word."

"You get a look at him?"

"I don't think I'll ever forget his face: olive complexion, clean shaven, but had very distinctive golden, yellow eyes, maybe originally from the Northern Tribal Areas, Pakistan or Afghanistan. The fellow who delivers the morning papers came by about the same time, but 1 don't think he saw him. The clean-up guy had disappeared by the time I got back out here."

"Could be anywhere by now," one of the policemen said. "We didn't see anybody like that on the way in."

"Doctor," Lt. Long said, "I'd like for you to come down to headquarters later and look at some mug shots. Lots of these guys are repeaters. Maybe we'll get lucky."

"Sure," JC said.

She continued, "Dr. Thomas, you took care of Patrolmen Rice last year. He was one of our people."

"Of course, I remember, really nice guy, he had a compound fracture of his distal femur from a wreck while chasing a bad guy. I got to know him pretty well. We had to operate several times, eventually got him back on his feet, no pun intended, but I'm afraid he'll probably have a limp for the rest of his life. Have you seen him lately?"

"He's back at work and doing well. Mainly desk work now, but he really sings your praises. The perp in that case also had a fracture. Did you take care of him?"

"Yeah, he had a broken arm, not much, didn't need surgery. It's a little harder to take care of the criminals, but that's part of the job I guess. What's he doing now?"

"He's doing five to seven for resisting and breaking and entering. Speaking of breaking and entering, we'll need to get some of our people to go over the scene here from the forensic standpoint. It's a long shot in a public area since everyone who's been here will leave some traces and prints, but we try."

By now it was about 6:30 in the morning and with the creeping gray light of day the shock of what had happened was beginning to wear off and other things were coming into focus. JC hadn't had much sleep lately. He needed a shave, a cup of coffee, and a change of clothes, but he was becoming more and more aware of Lt. Lauren Long. He didn't remember her name, but he did recall her image. She'd spent a lot of time with Rice when he was in the hospital. She'd seemed like a surrogate sister type helping out with the injured officer.

She was a little over five-three, five-four and flattered her business suit, even at this ungodly hour of the morning. She was a classy woman. Not a single brown hair was out of place around her face, which caught and held his gaze with very little make-up. She moved with a graceful walk and perfect posture. Just the first things any well-trained orthopaedic surgeon should notice.

The blue eyes seemed to twinkle on command and hid just enough of her soul to be interesting. Her smile was warm and frequent. She was not at all uncomfortable, but he was a bit

51

awkward when they bumped against each other while entering the office door together. JC guessed that she was probably pretty comfortable anywhere.

Lieutenant Long surveyed the scene while JC trudged back uphill to reality.

"Judging by this mess, I assume you're going to have to cancel some appointments today. You'll probably want to call your insurance company and you might want to consider changing your security system, although they probably did as good as any with this sort of crime. Adding some cameras around the entrance might be a help should this ever happen again."

"You'll want to look at your computers," she added. "These people are getting more sophisticated. Sometimes they can sell medical records and credit card information for a lot more then they get out of the cash drawer."

"I hadn't even thought of that," he admitted.

"If you and your office people could put together a list and let us know what all's missing, that would be a real help. Maybe you could come in later today, look at some photos and have us a list of the missing items by this afternoon. I know your time is important but I'd like to see you again tomorrow. You can call me before then if you think of anything else. Here's my card."

She had done this a time or two before and was relaxed and efficient, comfortable with being in charge. He couldn't think of a single thing to say, but he liked that part about seeing her again tomorrow. By then he would of course clean up and be prepared. He might even wear a tie. *When was his last hair cut anyway?*

"Thanks. See you then," JC managed as he watched Lt. Lauren Long return to her car.

It took all morning to tend to the details and clean up the mess in the office. By early afternoon he discovered that she was exactly right. There were no syringes or needles remaining in the cabinets and all of the laptops in the office were missing, including Charlie's.

Over the years, JC had accumulated various orthopaedic hardware that had been taken out of patients. He used these on occasion to demonstrate to prospective patients what their devices might look like. Now those implants were scattered all over the

52

floor. He couldn't really tell whether anything was missing. Why anybody would steal an old used prosthesis as a souvenir was beyond him, although if the thief decided to make a hood ornament out of a hip replacement, it sure would be an incriminating clue.

By nine-thirty with help from Jan and Julie, two of the office nurses who came in early, JC had made a thorough list of the missing items. They tried to reach all of the day's appointments, but a few who needed attention or medication refills showed up anyway. It was mid-afternoon by the time he took the list of missing items and went to the district headquarters to look at mug shots.

There were lots of photos to look at with one of the officers, but no match. There were some mean looking people in those books, but nothing even came close to that face he'd seen earlier. While he was waiting to work with the sketch artist, Patrolman Rice, now Sgt. Rice, came by the area and stopped.

"Dr. Thomas, didn't know you made house calls. What's up?"

"Somebody broke into our office last night and trashed the place. I saw the guy coming out, but he got away, so I've been looking at some of your friend's mug shots."

"Anybody in there look familiar?"

"Thought I saw some old patients, but otherwise no. They asked me to work with your artist when she gets back. Looks like you're moving pretty well. How are you feeling?"

"Knee's holding up okay long as I ride my bike. Who's in charge of your case?"

"Lt. Long," JC responded. "You still work with her?"

"No, not directly. Wish I did. You're lucky, she's the best."

"I guess we met back when you got hurt, but I just saw her again this morning at the office for a few minutes."

"Well, she's as nice as she is good-looking and ... " he paused. "Hello, Judy ... this is Dr. Thomas. He's the one got me back on my feet. You gonna do some drawing?"

"I am if you two will quit talking for a while," she smiled.

"Okay, okay," Sgt. Rice said, leaving. "Good to see you doc. Sorry for your problem. If I can help, just let me know."

JC worked with the talented sketch artist for over an hour

until they were both satisfied with a likeness. The image was still fresh and he hoped if he ever saw the man again, there were some armed guards around or some steel bars between.

JC did catch a glimpse of the Lieutenant behind the glass door of an office once or twice, but she didn't see him. He checked. *On the plus side, he did have a date, or, an appointment, to meet with her the next day.*

Finally after sixteen hours from leaving it, he drove home, stopping by his favorite place for a pepperoni and mushroom pizza, "thin crust please, to go."

By the time he got to his house, he was still pumped and not nearly as tired as he should have been. His mind was racing, but his body lagged behind a distant second. There was nothing interesting in the mail; no messages on the phone. After a shower, he sat down on the couch to eat his perfectly prepared Italian delicacy fresh from the establishment and turned on the news.

There was no report about the break-in. He really hadn't expected one, since they rarely report such things unless someone has been shot. The news anchor did say that the police had made no progress on the recent murders although he and his co-host were able to speculate for several minutes.

The flu was still raging and peace talks had resumed, but JC wasn't sure if they meant between the two political parties in Congress or between the factions overseas. A warming trend was expected by next week, and best of all, the point guard's ankle was "90 %." The weekend was coming.

Before turning in for the night, Dr. Thomas, the professor and scientist, made some conscious, well-reasoned, evidence-based decisions. He considered that his life was somehow lacking when the most exciting things in it were a robbery at his office and the ankle of an athlete he didn't even know.

All work and no play would apply to John, also. It had been a long time. His work had at one time been play, but lately work had become work. His social life was restricted to somebody's sister in town for the weekend or a group thing with the people from the hospital. Neither was a good choice to become involved with long term. He needed to branch out and look elsewhere. Maybe he should try to make some subconscious, unscientific, emotion based decisions for a change.

Chapter Ten

Burrowed deep in his basement, the hunter lay on the hard bed staring at the roof of his cave with his mind brooding on the empty result of the last night's activity. His thoughts were troubling, his mind was racing, and sleep had not come. His face had been seen, naked and open, marked by the American surgeon, and for that he had gained nothing. He had returned to his room again with no spoils. What he had desired, what he must soon possess, had not been found and time was growing short.

Time and freedom of movement, that's all that mattered to him. To carry out his commandments these two elements were paramount. Loss of life or limb, his own or anyone else's, made no difference—as long as he first executed his part of the plan. Self-sacrifice would come at some point, but only after he reached the goal. In fact, the goal required it.

While he had been too disturbed to sleep, he had closed and rested his watering eyes. He knew now that it had been a mistake to leave his brown lenses out believing no one would be at the building to observe. Why had the infidel doctor come to his business before the dawn?

He could not tolerate the error. He had been seen. He would learn, he would suffer, he would bear the irritation even in the darkness, a small pain compared to the others who had died for the cause. He knew he must conceal his eyes as they had always marked his face. They would come to know him very soon for his deeds and his passion. He would not be remembered for his likeness.

Perhaps better if he had killed the American at the office. There would be no one to identify him. It would not concern him at all to murder a witness. To swat a fly who became a pest. To kill an animal that had threatened, but this was not the time to attract any more attention from the homicide police.

There were so many burglaries unsolved in this district that he need not fear discovery for the break-in. The masses of infidels in this country who needed their drugs would steal again and again.

Even when they were captured, they were soon returned to the streets to continue their thievery--better the old way, the law of the mullahs, to chop off the hand of the one who steals with a large knife while the elders looked on. But these people were too weak, a nation of women. They would be easy to destroy. The police did not have time, there were not enough of them to find every thief. They would use many of their men to track one who murders, but they would never be able to catch him. He would be cunning and wary like the leopard. He would not be noticed again. Only a few lived in the community who might know his identity, and they were not the kind of people who would be seen talking with the authorities.

In fact, even those who might know his name didn't really know his identity. When he arrived in London years ago, the cell began calling him Basil. They noticed his pure dedication to duty and cause without regard for what they considered inconsequential —an individual's life or freedom. He saw the bigger vision. He behaved like a king.

Basil had not worn his beard for years and did not attend the mosque, but Allah would forgive him. He had made no friends and avoided the presence of the others in his small group. Except for the necessary trip to a store for food or a journey out in the night for killing and the harvest, he was invisible. He would look forward to meeting with the American doctor at a later time when he could take back what was his and not be concerned with another body to be found.

The stolen computers, along with the one belonging to the American, O'Reilly, remained in his backpack. If that contained dangerous bits of information, it would do the police no good now. He had little use for the electronic devices and the medicine prescription pads that he had stolen, but he would pass these along to the others. They could contain great amounts of information, he knew, and they might be very valuable to someone else. He was not concerned himself with the language of computers. He was the butcher who dressed the animals; the one who cut out the valuable parts and disposed of the waste.

Basil had never used any drugs. His family had sold the fruits of the poppy simply as a way to survive in his barren native land. The foreigners paid well for their produce. He did not know what might be in the glass vials he had taken. It was of no interest to him. He did know, however, that stealing these medicines and the syringes and needles would confirm this had been the act of a drug seeker, a large group among the infidels of this country. The police would not know of his other activities.

The hypodermics might have use to him later. There were some who put shots of liquid under the skin on their faces to make the chin look bigger, to thicken the nose, to change the line of the jaw, and therefore, to fool the cameras which were constantly searching for an image to match. He knew there were many traps waiting for him in the city.

Basil had seen the pictures of his brothers, the airplane takers, and knew the infidels were watching, but he had become more wary and would not be caught in their snares. Not now, but perhaps later, these needles would be needed and so they were kept in the metal cabinet along with his knives and a few other valuable articles.

Time was passing. He had already turned the number beside his front door - the signal had been sent. He must meet Kafeel to pass on the stolen goods and give directions for their next encounter. He could not change what had happened last night, but he knew what would bring him out of his somber mood. He must move on to his next prey. After kneeling on his rug and saying his prayers, he dressed himself and replaced his tinted lenses. On this journey he would be traveling through the increased security with metal detectors and cameras. He was careful to take the identification papers with his brown-eyed likeness, gloves and coveralls in the pockets of his coat, and to carry no weapons that could cause a warning. A powerful man, he had killed many with only his hands. When the American police used the words "armed and dangerous," they were not both needed to describe Basil. He had never been caught stealing, so he had both hands, and was always dangerous.

Walking through the neighborhoods, he was alone except for the occasional delivery vehicle passing on the street. He carried the backpack with the stolen computers to leave in the taxi. It was very cold and the wind was harsh in the narrow valleys of the city.

The tall buildings, like the rocky peaks of his youth, rose on either side as he made his way through the tight passageways and deserted canyons to arrive at the place on "U" street at the time he had chosen. There were no cameras here.

There was the cab waiting as his signal had directed. He opened the door and placed the pack on the floor. Basil then gave Kafeel a paper containing instructions for their next encounter. Not a word was spoken. Leaving the car and walking away, he was just another discharged fare in the big city, but this taxi and its driver would be unavailable to hire for some time to follow.

He next made his way through the windy valleys between the buildings to the tunnel under the ground where the powerful Metro prowled and took the Red Line to Union Station. Basil stood only a few blocks from the large white capital that had been close to destruction by a few men armed only with box cutters. His brothers had brought much pain, but they had not completed their mission. He would soon do a great deal better than that failed group.

Almost directly under the noses of those who ruled this country and The Great Satan, he left the subway in the large terminal and purchased his ticket for the outbound train with cash from the machine. He was only one of the masses who looked straight ahead and did not speak to the others. There were many men and women in the uniforms of police in the station, but he did not stand out in the rushing crowd.

Basil went through security with no difficulty, though the official did look closely. He boarded the coach for the two hour trip south. Headphones in place like most of the other travelers, it was easy to blend in and avoid notice. With his eyes half closed, slit-like, planning, he preferred no sound coming to his ears, but he watched every movement of the herd.

Once he arrived at his destination, the man with the brown eyes and the olive skin departed the train and took a twisted, winding route through the town. No one followed. The hunter buttoned his coat with the paper cover-ups in the pockets and walked some distance to a working class neighborhood.

The air was warmer here and the trees were showing green, the Prophet's color. This was the green of his flag that also

58

contained the open Book. These people would come to know these symbols very soon, he thought, as he walked among them. His eyes were alert and darting, constantly observing, while he, himself, was invisible. There was little difficulty finding his way. The map had been very accurate, and he had followed much more difficult trails.

With no security system in place, it was easy to enter through a basement window of the small house once the early darkness of winter fell. He could hear the two occupants moving and talking to each other above. Like the snake, barely breathing, he could wait unmoved for hours and then strike suddenly.

After their evening meal was finished, he heard the man leave to watch the television in another room. The wife was left cleaning in her small kitchen. He could hear her moving about, turning the sink on and off, cleaning dishes and putting them away, opening the refrigerator door. He steadied his mind; time to act.

Basil climbed up the few stairs behind the small and fragile creature. In three quick strides he came upon her as she looked out the window finishing her work. No one could hear the cracking noise when he broke her neck; inaudible over the television's drone. He lowered her lifeless body to the floor without a sound.

He waited, low and coiled, scarcely breathing and easily out of sight until the man came into the kitchen. Before the husband could reach his bride of thirty years, the snake struck with the same deadly force. Like the crime against his wife, few clues evidenced the violence wrought. Not a drop of blood appeared.

Basil had put on the shoe covers and coveralls before he entered in the basement. He was not concerned that a footprint or an open window would be found, but he did want to leave little evidence of an intruder inside and certainly no damning signs of his own presence.

He easily carried both of the bodies to the garage and placed them in the rear of the victims' truck out of sight. They had driven a dirty green pickup with the shell of a camper over the bed. The truck was old and scratched, but there was plenty of room in the back. It was an ideal place to conceal the corpses and their belongings.

He was sure to include the woman's purse and the recently

used passports. He even packed a small suitcase with the medicines from the cabinet and a change of clothes for each of them from the drawers. He took a large sharp knife, probably the same one used to fix their last meal, from the kitchen. He checked for the flashlight in the glove compartment of their vehicle. It had strong working batteries, which he might need later.

The killer then opened the garage after looking outside. There was no one about on the dark street watching as he backed the vehicle out and closed the door. He drove for an hour into the wilderness, to the chosen isolated place.

Before exiting the vehicle, the hunter looked around for any recent tracks or signs of activity in the area. Only indications of Kafeel carrying out Basil's instructions appeared. Feeling secure to proceed, Basil continued on with his plans.

The assassin removed the bodies from the back of the truck and harvested their valuable parts in short order. It was cold, but he did not feel that as he worked quickly. The knife was sharp, and with his skills of butchery, he quickly took what he needed and carefully packaged the pieces in plastic bags he took from their home.

He placed the remaining parts, along with the woman's purse and suitcase, in the hole that the courier had prepared. He scraped the dirt back over the shallow grave with the shovel that Kafeel left there after he put the coveralls, knife and gloves in with the bodies. Finally, he placed the shovel in a large trash sack to take along with him. Returning to the victim's pickup with new shoe covers and gloves, Basil knew there would be no blood, no dirt, and no little traces to be found.

His work was almost done. He drove to the designated church parking lot with no lights and no security cameras, which was half-way back to the district. As he left the vehicle with the fruits of his harvest inside and started his trek back to a different train station, he saw the shadow of another man waiting in the distance.

Basil knew the courier would dispose of the vehicle and properly store the valuables he had collected. They had not been seen together and now he would board the train for the return trip. Even if he were selected for a random search, there would be no trace of his work. The plans had gone well, and he was confident he would succeed. It would be some time before Mr. and Mrs. Smith would be reported missing. It was not uncommon for them to take off in their dirty green pickup truck, spur of the moment, for a camping trip or a hike. Their friends knew that they had always enjoyed hiking together in the woods. In fact, that was the reason they had recently traveled overseas and had their painful hips replaced.

Chapter Eleven

On the third floor of the district police headquarters was the homicide division. Tim and LB sat in a small conference room cluttered with papers, phones, and monitors to review the recent deaths and mutilations. This was where most of the work got done.

One wall held a board with the black scrawl of a timeline for the three murders, while another contained a map of the city with pins marking the crime scenes. Soft drink cans, coffee cups, and half eaten snacks decorated the table. No self-respecting homicide detective should ever run low on caffeine or sugar or stop for a decent meal; the job is too pressing.

"Tim, you still dating that girl from Channel Five Nightly News?" LB asked as they waited for the Chief.

"If you mean Karen Armstrong, we're only friends from high school."

"So she's still in high school then?"

"Of course not! She finished community college in three years in the top ninety percent of her class. But we're not really dating, we're just good friends", Tim said as the Chief walked in.

His cold was getting better. There was no more sneezing, just an occasional cough and that shortness of breath and tired feeling that came with the effort of standing all the way up and walking all the way across a room. With a red irritated nose and chapped lips, he spoke in his still raspy voice.

"I'll only take a few minutes. I want to review where we are now. Feel free to butt right in if I leave something out or if a little light comes on."

No lights came on yet, so the Chief continued.

"The first girl has been identified as Peggy Dow, aged thirty-one. She came over from Pittsburgh for a training session but never made it to the hotel. Her two children were spending the week in Cleveland with their father, who reported her missing when she didn't show to pick them up. She'd been gone for eight days by then. They were divorced, he remarried two years ago, but they still talked to each other when they had to."

"Confirmed!" Tim said. "The ex was two hours away with the kids at the presumed time of death," pointing to the timeline on the board. "They shared custody and if she were out of the picture he would have saved on child support and gotten both the kids full time - some motive there, so we can't rule out a murder for hire."

"You think he paid somebody to kill his ex," LB asked, "and then got the man to kill the other two just to throw us off?"

Tim replied, "Well, I've seen stranger things so we'll keep the former husband on the list. But, personally, I think we're looking for a crazy sexual pervert. A real psychopath on a random killing spree."

LB, trying to spare the Chief's voice, took up, "Ms. Dow has been described by her friends as a pretty, outgoing young woman of average build without an enemy in the world. So far we can't find any evidence that she knew anybody who lived in D.C., and there is nothing to suggest that she came here to meet up with a friend from out of town. We've been through her relatives, co-workers and most of the people who were attending school with her. She was taking night classes to become a legal assistant."

"She have any previous record?" Tim asked. "Drug seeker who picked the wrong guy looking for a hit, sex for sale, anything illegal?"

"No history of drugs, only a few minor traffic citations. Looks like an All-American mom who just happened to be in the wrong place." LB answered.

Tim was pointing to where the body was found on the map, while LB continued.

"We think she may have been confused and exited the metro at a stop too soon coming in from Reagan National and ended up having to walk to her hotel. Body was found about half-way between the two stations near where Tim's pointing. So far no usable security video data once she left the train, but we probably should review those tapes again now that we know who she is."

"Here's a photo from two months ago with her kids," LB went on. "Take a look. So far we can't find anyone who didn't like her and no one with any kind of real motive."

She shuffled some papers and, with the Chief's nod, continued.

"The M.E. has officially called it a homicide and the manner of death was manual strangulation with a lot of force. Trace of glove powder on her neck, but no usable prints. Large sharp instrument, not serrated, was used to remove her breasts and lacerate her abdomen. Looks like that happened postmortem. Ten separate cuts in the stomach and chest area. Blood work was negative except for some small amount of Xanex that she had a prescription for."

The hoarse voice of the Chief struggled again. "Once the missing persons report came in on her, we were able to come close from the pictures, even though her face had been badly cut. Her dental records and prints confirmed the identity."

"We're still working on the second one," Tim said, as he pointed to the timeline on the board. "Estimated to be five six, five seven, about one hundred and fifty pounds. Probably twenty-five to thirty-five with no scars or tattoos. Looks like she was choked to death, just like the first one. Her face was so slashed up it's going to be hard to ID her from a picture, and so far, no match with missing persons. We don't even know if she lived here or not."

"The body was found right here," Tim pointed, "about two miles from the first. Her boobs were hacked off. Looks like the whole front of her chest in one piece, probably with the same knife, and the killer took all that part of her and her underwear with him, just like the other two. Lots of deep slashes in her stomach after she was dead. Here's her photo from the scene. They think it's just random cuts, but I'll bet there's a message or some sort of a symbol carved in there. This one kinda' looks like a cross. Both her hands were chopped off and taken away, so no prints on this one, but she did have full mouth dental implants, brand new ones, that we're trying to match. So far nothing from the local dentists. I bet she was from out of town, too."

He quickly added, "Her blood showed some traces of oxycodone, probably from the dental work, but nothing illegal. The M.E. could tell her gums still showed some signs of trauma in the last month or six weeks when her teeth were done."

Tim went to the board and added "dentist" on the timeline.

The Chief said, "I've been reviewing the crime scene photographs on the third woman. It looks like her assailant was able to get real close and killed her right there on the street. There were no signs of a struggle. She was probably dragged into the alley, causing her boots to come off. Judging by the blood patterns, that's where the mutilation took place. Similar to one and two, but this time he severed her neck and took everything from there up in addition to her chest and hands."

Tim moved the pin on the map just a bit to identify the exact spot.

"There was a small light bulb over her on the side of the building that was working the day before," Chief Lane said, "but it was broken after he was finished. There were a few shards on top of the body. Some consolation that she was most likely dead before he began slashing her. At least we know her heart wasn't pumping, so she was spared that pain just like the other girls. We don't have a cause of death on her yet, tox screen negative so far, but it's early, still cooking. I assume her lethal injury was either to the neck like the others or a blow to the head, but we don't know for sure, being as how there's no head."

The Chief continued, "It looks like the time of death in all three of these was somewhere between eight at night and midnight and they occurred on three different days of the week."

"Probably works during the daytime," Tim put in. "Lives alone so he can get out at night whenever he wants to. He's able to get real close. Nobody heard any screams, no signs of a struggle. Might be dressed like somebody they could trust - maybe like a policeman or something."

"One thing that strikes me in all three of these is that there's been no physical evidence of forcible rape, no foreign body fluids, PSA negative for semen in the area," LB said. "You'd have to think there's a lot of anger and sexual aggression with the complete removal of the breasts and the slashing of the other areas."

"He probably took the parts home and no telling what he's doing with them there," Tim said. "He's progressing, getting more violent every time. With the next one he may start cannibalism, if he hasn't already. The other thing I'm looking for is for him to send us a letter or a body part. These guys are so egotistical they just can't help bragging about their crimes, daring us to catch them. He might even go directly to the press, so I've asked them to let us know if something turns up. I wouldn't be surprised if he hadn't taken some photographs of these victims. We should alert the photo shops."

LB wondered if Tim had entered the digital camera age yet.

"Better stick with what we know," the Chief said.

"Yeah, that's right. I remember Sherlock Holmes said to use the data. Make the conclusion fit the facts, not the other way around." Tim helpfully translated from the original English for the benefit of the group.

LB slowly rolled her eyes as she looked skyward.

"Did we get anywhere with the neighborhood interviews?" the Chief intervened.

"We've gotten several reports of suspicious people in the areas – nothing confirmed," LB said. "We're going to continue to follow up, but I'm not real hopeful. We've got four people calling to confess, although they weren't able to give any details on these cases and two of them have called before on other homicides."

The Chief said, "Yeah, I did hear that on the news. I wonder how the press got hold of it?"

For a moment, there was total silence in the room and Tim was even quieter than usual as he continued to study the map with his back turned.

"Well, it certainly looks like the same M.O., and forensics tells me that the cut marks could have all come from the same sharp instrument," the Chief paused. "Looks like we probably have a true serial killer in the city. Profiler's working this up, but we don't have much to go on. Any other questions…? Anything to add … ? Okay then, we've got our assignments, so let's roll up our sleeves and get to work."

As they started to leave the room, the Chief said, "I guess I'd better talk with the press, again. They're starting to speculate and this is becoming a real heater. We need to come up with something pretty soon before there's a fourth one."

The door was opening when he added, "By the way, I think it's a good idea that anything going to the press should come through me first."

Chapter Twelve

At the same time on the floor below, JC was being shown into Lt. Long's office. He noticed all the cops he passed along the way had on side arms, like stethoscopes on a cardiologist, and they were all in a hurry. JC had on his blazer and dress slacks, open collared shirt, and a fresh haircut.

Lauren, a keen observer with an eye for detail, came forward to meet him with a genuine smile. He'd dressed up. Probably going out to some nice restaurant with one of the nurses later on, she surmised, while she herself was planning to work late and have pizza at the office—pepperoni with extra cheese.

She extended her right hand. The left, JC confirmed, was without a ring and held a red Coke can, not the diet kind. From what he could see, he suspected she never needed the one that came in the silver can. The Lieutenant was even better looking in the daylight than he remembered from the morning before. She wore just a touch of lipstick, but nothing much else for make-up that he could tell. Her hair was pulled back in a pony-tail, something quick that didn't need much attention. Pretty common to nurses, doctors, and apparently cops—those whose urgent presence was often more important than their appearance.

As she offered him a chair in front of the neat desk and retreated back to her seat, he observed her reasonable one and a half inch heels, slim ankles and well-proportioned calves, just the things any well-trained orthopaedic surgeon would have observed. Her desk was old and scratched—no tax payer money wasted—but organized, with a few photos on top. He tried not to look too closely…but did that one show her with a handsome man about her age?

"Well, how are you doing?" she asked. "This really puts a crimp in your schedule I suspect."

"I'm ok, but this is a little different situation," he said. "We're about to get the office back in shape."

"Yes, I can imagine. We've been doing a bit of background. Let's see, Dr. Thomas, you've been practicing in that office for almost four years now?"

"Yes, that's right, and most people call me JC."

"I notice you spent some time in the military."

"Yeah, I was fortunate enough to do some of my Ortho residency training there. Then I was stationed over in Turkey for a few years before I came back to D.C. and started private practice."

"You've got four partners in with you, isn't that right?"

"We've been in a group for over three years now. It spreads out the call and the office expenses a little bit."

"I've looked at the list of your employees and we ran a quick check on them. Nothing to be worried about there, but we had to look. Sometimes these are inside jobs. The cleaning crew all check out. The man you saw wasn't on their payroll, and nobody seems to know anything about him."

"The way he looks with those fierce eyes, I'd be surprised if anybody wasn't too afraid to hire him."

"Well, besides syringes, needles, prescription pads and computers," she continued, "you come up with anything else missing?"

"No, nothing we can tell. He could have taken some of the removed metal implants that we keep around for demonstration. They were scattered all over the place, but we don't keep a count of them," JC answered.

"We haven't heard anything about counterfeit prescriptions on your pads, any of the pharmacists contact you yet?"

"No, we're in the process of changing those pads and we try to do most of our prescribing electronically now, anyway. Fortunately we have the medical records and patient files backed up off site. I can't imagine what might happen to that information if it were to fall into the wrong hands. I did alert our data security company. We had to change all our passwords."

"That area of stolen data and identification theft is beyond our scope, but we'll let you know if something turns up. Have you thought of any patients that might have reason to do something like this?"

"No one that stands out. Of course we do see drug seekers like all the other offices and prisoners come back from time to time in follow-up from the emergency rooms, but they're always accompanied by a uniformed officer. I guess they might have seen something while they were there."

"We'll try to match any appointments with people that have been incarcerated recently in our system," she said as she made a note.

"Any of your partners have any suspicions?"

"No, not really, we talked about it, but nothing really jumped out."

"Any business or marital difficulties?"

"No, I'm not married."

"I meant with your partners," she smiled.

"Oh ... no, nothing that would lead to this sort of thing."

"No matches in the mug shots. That sketch is pretty good, though. Those eyes are really distinctive...and a bit threatening."

"Yeah, it's hard to do justice to it on paper, but that's a face 1 don't think I'll ever forget."

"We'll be working on this from several different angles and get back to you when we turn up something. Sometimes they try to sell the stolen goods or they try again somewhere else and get caught," she said. "Maybe we'll get lucky.”

She looked him in the eye as she spoke, "Now, JC ... I've asked you a lot of questions. Is there anything you'd like to ask me?"

"Well, there is one thing."

"Shoot."

"One of my partners takes care of the basketball team, and he gave me two tickets for this Saturday night. I was wondering if you'd like to go?"

Lieutenant Long was a trained professional. The others in the office would no longer invite her to their poker games, but this time she knew she had blinked.

Did he just ask her for a date? They probably don't have time for a class in social skills in medical school. She had tons of work to do and watching big, tall, sweaty men chase after a little rubber ball while a crowd of people screamed their heads off was not exactly her cup of tea. They had, after all, just met.

Did his voice just change octaves when he asked her out? That was kind of refreshing--certainly a different approach than her swaggering, lying, egotistical ex. All of this was processing rapidly while she said, "I ... uh ... "

"It's a really big game," he said, struggling to keep his voice steady. "You might have heard it being talked about on the news—it's for first place and a play-off birth."

She opened her mouth to offer an excuse, but was surprised at the words that came out.

"Well, you know, that might be fun."

He brightened and quickly closed the deal.

"Maybe I could pick you up about six, do you live around here somewhere?"

"I usually come in and try to get some things done on Saturday," she said. "Why don't you just meet me here?"

She was forced to add, "I know you understand with the kind of work that you do, but sometimes we get "Urgents" at the last minute."

He understood, but chose not to think about it. How often had he used that same phrase in similar situations?

Her beeper was chirping again as they said goodbye. She promised to call if she found out plans had to be changed.

As he bounced out of the office and down the hall, Lauren smiled. Dr. John Christopher Suave had completely forgotten to ask what color dress she'd be wearing. She wouldn't be at all surprised if he showed up with a wrist corsage and a box of chocolates.


Chapter Thirteen

JC swung and landed a hard right hand on the "OFF" switch before the alarm had a chance to begin its thundering barrage of blows to the midsection of his ear. The allure of the hard plastic snooze bar had cracked and faded almost overnight. He'd seen it coming for a while; it was time to move on. The muted glow of the clock's smiling face reminded him of the soft pink shades of sunrise over the ocean and whispered that he might want to get up from bed or maybe not. He had plenty of time.

It was Friday. And this particular Friday would be followed by Saturday and Sunday. A short workday with no ER call plus a huge basketball game tomorrow that he would personally attend with a certain shapely police lieutenant for company made arising from bed very easy for JC.

The coffee was especially rich, none of that bitter after taste, and the beads of water from the shower head were all exactly the same size and warm temperature as they massaged his shoulders. He slipped into slacks, an open-collar dress shirt and a pullover sweater. He never wore a tie and rarely a sports coat. In fact, that blazer he had on yesterday was looking a little faded. How long had he had that thing? Was that the one he got for the Super Bowl XXXIV party? And which number Super Bowl was next anyway?

He was supposed to be off work after his morning clinic. All the hospitals were full, and there were no beds to accommodate elective surgery patients. He had to call and cancel two scheduled operations for the afternoon due to the bed shortage, and all the out-patient slots had been taken for a week. Maybe he should use the time to look for a new coat?

The car started easily. The windshield was clear as JC backed out of the short driveway. *Maybe the garage could wait 'til it was warmer,* he thought. *Spring cleaning must be a tradition for some good reason.*

Once out in the street, he turned and drove in front of his home on Ridgeview Avenue before continuing on down his street a few blocks past the convenience store to the entry ramp of the beltway. He moved to the house some three years ago. Even though it was a longer drive, he enjoyed the feeling of being removed from the bustle of downtown.

The traffic seemed especially light this morning. The roads were clear and the other commuters had improved their driving skills considerably over the past few days. As one of the large green moving vans slowed and signaled him to merge, JC crossed over on a Mayflower before he entered Washington proper. He noticed that the lights were restored around the tall white monument, which was visible in the distance at the west end of the mall. Maybe he'd drive around the tidal basin after work to see if anything had changed.

The sky was still gray, but at least there'd been no more snow overnight. He listened to the local news on the way, trying to find at least three interesting topics for conversation, apart from the subject of medicine, by tomorrow night. Also, if he excluded the potentially dangerous areas of sex, politics, and religion, that didn't leave much around Washington to talk about.

The radio informed him that the number of flu cases had remained stable. It looked like the worst was over, and the hospitals might soon get a bit of relief from their overflow status; nothing new to report on the recent homicides; record crowd expected for the ball game tomorrow night and spring was on the way. That was all well and good but so far all he had come up with was sports and weather for tomorrow night's small talk.

The gate had been repaired and he parked easily. Plenty of spaces today in the doctors' lot, and it was probably worth the contribution to the Foundation to get into the oversubscribed reserve area for physicians. As he walked around the back of the car, he remembered that the hip prostheses he had taken out last Tuesday, as well as several discs, were still in his trunk. At some point he would need to talk to Charlie about electively exchanging his other hip before it had a chance to fail, but he thought it best to give him a month or so to recover from this surgery.

Sometime in the next week or two JC might want to call one of the older, more experienced professors at the University and let them take a look at the removed stem out of academic curiosity. Maybe that design had come and gone before his time. He'd also need to remember to store O'Reilly's copied disc in the garage.

After entering the hospital, he stopped to say hello to the nurses on the floor. Some of them would be off this weekend and they were looking forward to resting and spending time with their families. Others of the staff were on their ninth straight day and they would be on the job again in the morning.

Still others had been working double shifts and were exhausted. Although they would do a good job for their patients, they were too busy and too frazzled for chit-chat. *Avoid them if possible today*, JC noted. *Rx a dozen glazed and a dozen chocolate covered for tomorrow morning.* It wasn't the cure, but it might help with the symptoms until the influenza epidemic was over.

*Time to make rounds in the following precise order: critical patients first, possible discharges next, and save Mrs. Sherman for last.* Since there had been no crises overnight with his people, JC could skip category one this morning.

Room 517: Charlie O'Reilly. The chart looked good. His temperature was down and his blood count was stable. The physical therapists were teaching him how to walk with his new hip, and JC paused and watched from the door for a minute. The crutches were flying. The gown gaping open in back wasn't bothering anybody and the safety belt the therapist held around his waist was functioning more like a choke collar on a puppy to keep him from running.

"Charlie, try to slow down a little," JC said, trying to hide a smile. "I'm glad you're feeling so well, but remember you are still weak."

"Okay, doc, I'll try to remember. I've had a lot of practice with these crutches lately."

"Yeah, the PT people say they want you to help them teach the other patients."

"Hey, doc, I been thinking. I don't need any more pain shots and I sure as hell don't need anymore IV's. I've been up and down to pee all night. Nothing personal, I really like all these people, but can't I go on home today?"

JC suspected that the man probably wanted to have a drink of something besides diluted hospital fruit juice from the cardboard carton or the lukewarm ice water through that bent straw.

"I'm real sorry about that break-in at your office," Charlie said. "The nurses told me all about it. Don't worry about the laptop. I got everything backed-up on my desktop at the office, and home owners should cover it. I might need a police report though."

"I'm sorry about that," JC said. "We should have a copy of the report by the time you come in the office. Now, Charlie, if we let you go today, promise you'll try and stay out of trouble this time?"

"You can count on me, doc. First thing I'm going to do is get some better shoes."

The nurses arranged home health visits and a follow up appointment; the appropriate prescriptions were signed-- Charlie was already on his way out the door. JC saw all of his other patients and there were no problems. They were working with PT. Blood counts were stable and blood thinners were appropriately dosed. Two more were ready for discharge. The hospital administrator and the insurance carriers would be pleased.

*Finally. No more stalling. The post op total knee in Room 503: Mrs. Sherman.* She was constantly complaining about the hospital facilities and the uncomfortable bed. The nursing staff was slow to answer her light. Things had gotten significantly worse since her last two admissions here. She was not getting enough pain medicine, and the food was always cold and needed salt. She thought she should stay for at least three more days. JC was sympathetic. She was right about the bed and the salt. As he sat down and listened patiently, he noticed that there were no balloons, no flowers, no green and yellow Crayola hearts drawn on a piece of lined tablet paper.

Maybe his good mood would rub off if he sat there a few more minutes and let her vent. *Did the frown fade just a little bit the longer he listened and responded with an occasional "uh-huh or hmmm"?*

After a while he said, "Well, let me see what I can do. Why don't we just take it a day at a time? Work hard with the therapist today and I'll see you again in the morning."

As he was finishing the ever-expanding paperwork, one of the nurses asked, "Dr. Thomas, you gonna get to go to the ballgame tomorrow night?"

JC knew her well, a great nurse if not a little chatty, at significant risk of developing overused-tongue syndrome. He was pretty sure she had been working at the desk the day Dr. Short had invited him out to dinner with his sister-in-law.

"Yeah, I was lucky enough to get two tickets. Taking a real nice new girl. I don't think you know her though. She doesn't work on this floor."

There were some good reasons why doctors were never

allowed behind the closed doors when the nurses reported to each other at the change of shifts or during their short breaks. Some days the conversations were probably boring, but today there might be a little more to talk about, he thought as he smiled and said goodbye.

*****************

Not everyone in Washington was enjoying life this Friday as much as JC and Charlie. The custodian, Al, was miserable -- throbbing headache, temperature, chills, a runny nose and aching all over. He couldn't remember ever feeling this bad before from the flu.

To add to his woes, there was a sore on the back of his wrist that was enlarging. It started with a scratch five days ago at work and should be almost well by now, not getting worse. He got these scrapes all the time and they always healed, but this thing was now as black as tar and bigger than a Euro. It was deep and irritating and starting to slough off the surrounding skin.

He had to be at work today. One of the biggest events of the year was planned for the next day, and he needed to personally oversee things in the building through tomorrow night. Once that was over, Al was planning a long vacation followed by a career change. The travel arrangements had already been made.

After his morning prayers, he made sure the cuff of his uniform covered the lesion on his wrist, and struggled out the door toward the downtown area where he was currently employed.

*****************

At JC's office, his morning clinic was busier than usual, but then it seemed like it always was. A number of work-in patients who had been canceled on the day of the burglary needed to be seen before the weekend. There were also a great many phone messages that his nurse, Jan, had done a good job of screening, but some he had to call back himself. There were prescriptions that needed his evaluation for refills and follow-ups that needed to be arranged. There were off work excuses and Medicare forms that had to be signed.

Due to the older age of the population group he frequently treated, it was not uncommon for some of his ex-patients to appear in the obituary columns from time to time. Jan and Julie went through these in the newspapers, and JC made a point to personally sign a sympathy card to the families. Some of these people had become real friends over time, and he would miss them.

The nurses brought to his attention that day the printed obituary of a certain "Dr. Moore" who had been a plastic surgeon practicing in the Virginia suburbs. JC didn't know him and couldn't remember ever having met the man. He had no family listed. He had enjoyed traveling, and had been on vacation in the eastern Mediterranean when he was lost at sea two weeks ago. Further details were not available. A small memorial service would be held next Tuesday.

Skipping lunch, JC finished up the details at the office by early afternoon. He wished the staff a pleasant weekend away from work and set out for the shops around DuPont Circle in search of a new sports coat.

There he discovered that blue blazers were getting a bit more difficult to find, apparently because of their popularity. After trying several stores, however, he found one off the rack that the clerk assured him fit "just fine." *Three buttons were making a comeback*. He agreed with the salesman after trying it on and checking in the mirror, front, sides, sleeves. It wasn't every day that he bought a new coat.

All the shopping made him really hungry. About all he'd had to eat lately was pizza, and he missed lunch again today. He needed a good balanced meal. Since he was in the area already, he went in to one of the many nice restaurants and treated himself to a giant cheeseburger with both mayonnaise and mustard along with a large order of fries. While enjoying a Danish for desert and awaiting some other pastries to take home, it struck him. He'd forgotten to think of conversation topics for tomorrow night, something that would interest Lt. Long. He had walked right past the bookstore. He had homework to do.

JC spent over an hour browsing through the "mystery and

detective" section of books with a cup of high dollar coffee. He looked at a lot of selections and finally settled on a novel about the psychologist investigator that used to work for the D.C. Police Department--should be right up her alley. He also found a classic detective book with the colorful prose of Raymond Chandler.

The drive home was easy and, after seeing no new messages, JC hung the coat up in his closet. There was plenty of room in there to let it hang separately without touching anything else since it was just him now. The other closets in his three-bedroom house were empty and had been for some time, which produced a quiet, peaceful atmosphere. JC turned on the TV to watch the news.

Tonight, at random, Channel Five flooded the living room as a jelly filled pastry disappeared. He didn't learn much new from the program, but he did notice that the enthusiastic co-anchor looked quite familiar. JC didn't recognize her personally, but she reminded him of a friendly and chatty cheerleader he had dated in high school twenty years ago. He remembered her with the kind of special fondness everyone reserves for their 'first'. She had been beautiful and even though he had been told he was good looking, he had most definitely not been jock material. He'd been voted "Most Likely to Succeed" by his classmates. She must have had some kind of weird thing for science geeks.

Weather-- Continued clear and cold.

Sports-- The game was tomorrow. Ankle: 92%. *What else could be said?* It took ten minutes and JC listened to every word.

*Okay*, he thought as he turned the TV off, *time to get to work*. If he started now, by tomorrow night he would be able to discuss the characters of both Alex Cross and Philip Marlowe.


Chapter Fourteen


JC pulled up outside the district headquarters twenty minutes early. It was a cold, crisp, still night and static electricity was abundant in the air. Things were definitely going his way when he found one of those "Two Hour Limit" parking places right in front of the building next to the six vacant handicapped slots. That should be plenty of time to pick up Lauren and head on out for the game without getting a citation or having to find change for a dollar inside the station.

He pulled his car into place squarely between the white lines. Knowing he was on camera already, he resisted the urge to wave. JC made a final check of the front passenger area which he'd cleaned and washed before leaving home. There hadn't been anybody over there in a long time, just groceries and fast food sacks. The only thing worse than a pizza receipt drawing extra attention by sticking to the rear of a lady's dress would have been a large damp spot for a cop to sit. *Good*, he thought, as he patted the seat. *Dry as a bone.*

It was the third trip to this station in the last few days and he was beginning to feel at home. He took the stairs, two at a time, rather than wait for the cable-stressing elevator. He opened the door onto the second floor: Robbery Division.

This was the first time he'd been here after dark, however, and the dimly lit, off-white and thinly painted waiting area took him by surprise. It was deserted. He'd guessed that police headquarters was similar to the hospital emergency room business model in that most of the really good customers didn't show up until somewhat later on Saturday nights.

The uniformed sergeant at the front desk was new to him. JC would have remembered if he'd seen this man before. The fellow was so big and muscular in appearance that his nightstick looked more like a large pencil. He had to be a huge part of some offensive line in the NFL who was doing a service to the community during the off-season as a police officer.

The left guard looked up from studying his playbook behind a bank of monitors as JC approached, and in a voice that matched his frame declared, "You must be Dr. Thomas."

"Yeah ... how'd you know?"

"Lieutenant said about five-ten, one sixty-five, one seventy with sandy hair, maybe wearing a blue sports coat," he said. "Besides, some of the other guys here were talking after they saw you leave her office the last time. She wouldn't ever say anything, but the bet was you'd show up with a box of donuts."

"You think that'd help?" JC said, smiling.

"Nah, she never eats 'em," the sergeant grinned, "but we do.

Maybe next time."

The man looked like one of those ten thousand plus calorie a day types that you wanted protecting your blind side if you were planning to throw it deep. *In fact*, JC thought, *it wouldn't hurt to have his help with any kind of pass you wanted to make.*

"Chocolate or jelly-filled?" he said.

"Both," his new teammate reasoned. "Anyway, doc, she just came out to check and said to tell you she'd be about fifteen or twenty minutes late. Said she was real sorry. Something urgent came up and if you wanted to go on without her she'd understand."

JC looked at his watch, not trusting the huge clock mounted above his new teammate's clean-shaven head. It was still early. They would only miss part of the warm-ups and probably still make the anthem if they left in the next fifteen or twenty minutes.

"Guess I'll just wait here if that's okay."

"Good call, doc. She's worth the wait, and you'll have plenty of time."

"Thanks, I owe it all to my offensive line."

The guard had probably heard that once or twice before, but grinned again anyway.

"First part of those games aren't ever too good. It's funny, we didn't know she was a fan--thought she just worked all the time."

The sergeant probably knew a lot more than he was saying, but then that went along with his real job as an offensive lineman. He returned to his studies as JC took a seat in the empty waiting area.

He thought, unfortunately this same thing must happen a lot at his office even though he tried to stay on time. Patients arrived all dressed up and ready to see the doctor. At least, they'd put on their most uncomfortable new underwear. They'd come in early and anxious, then have to sit there and wait. There were some things that just couldn't be scheduled in either of their jobs: the "Urgents" that demanded immediate attention.

Still, he did get a little fidgety once he discovered the red second hand running a stop and go route around the big official clock. There was not even an old copy of "Police Gazette" to flip through. They probably had been lifted by the very same criminals in the magazines' stories. At least nobody stole "Today's Health" from his office. Some of them had been sitting there unguarded for over three years.

Looking for anything to pass the time, JC studied the only other wall decorations in the taxpayer furnished room. There was a touched-up color picture of the mayor, whom he recognized, and another picture of a man in uniform with a lot of stars. He must be the Chief of Police. He squinted to read the name under the thin fake wood border surrounding the photo, but he couldn't quite make it out.

He turned next to examine the notices of equal employment and the OSHA requirements, which had been formatted by those same people that made eye charts. The text was so small toward the bottom that it could only be read by a plaintiff's lawyer wearing bifocals. The same attorneys who could read the "Probably not Related" section under "Possible Adverse Reactions" on the drug package inserts.

After twenty-seven minutes, the Lieutenant appeared at her door and JC's visual acuity improved dramatically. He hadn't fully appreciated how great she could look. Maybe it had been the formless business suit at 5:30 in the morning or maybe it had been his lack of sleep, because now, dressed in a tan knee length skirt and a brown wool sweater, he was afraid she might be looking for someone else. Her outfit was fitted just close enough that he could tell there was no protective Kevlar hiding underneath.

JC had time to see the perfect position of her small patellae and the tendons just below them leading on down the well-aligned tibiae to her ankles and the two and a half inch heels, just things any well-trained orthopaedic surgeon would notice, before her face caused him to forget that's what he was.

She had that red Coke can for a prop in her left hand, thereby eliminating some of the awkward greeting options, but she offered her right and their fingers met somewhere between a formal handshake and an old Beatle's song.

"I'm so sorry for running late, but I just couldn't help it," she said with sad blue eyes. "Can we still make it to the game?"

"Sure, it won't hurt to miss a few minutes anyway."

"If you want to, we can take my car. Of course, we can't

79

use the siren," she said as his face lit up, "but sometimes it comes in handy with traffic and parking."

"That'd be great. They give you your own car?"

"After you've been here for a while. They must'a gotten a good deal on black Fords this year. You might leave the keys with the desk just in case they need to move yours."

She turned to the sergeant. "Darren, would you mind?"

"Sure, toss 'em over."

"It's parked right out front. "

"Blue sedan, clean seats. We saw you drive up. I'll take care of it. Now, you two have a good time, but doc," he said, looking JC in the eye. "We expect her back here by midnight."

She led him down the stairs and pointed out her four-door sedan. They all looked alike to JC. Once they were inside and the seat belts were secure, she headed out of the space, through the underground lot, and turned onto the street. The Lieutenant drove a little faster than he would, but she was a pro and they were running late. She seemed distracted, so JC thought it would be a good time to work into the detective theme.

"You been with the department for a while now?"

"About twelve years; since I finished school. My dad was on the force and had to take a medical retirement. My older brother, you might have seen his picture on my desk, is a pilot. He flies overseas a lot now so I decided to carry on the family tradition. I really enjoy the work, but probably like your business, there are times when things come up that just demand your attention. That can be really frustrating as far as a personal life is concerned."

"Yeah, I can relate. Big case just come up?"

She hesitated just a second before she launched, "Unbelievable! It'll be all over the news pretty soon, so we can talk about it. In fact, I need to talk to you about it if you don't mind."

He didn't, but the implication peaked his curiousity.

"They've turned up six suspected cases of respiratory anthrax in the city, one in a 15-year old boy. Briefing said years ago people used to get that from bad meat, but our food supply now is so well regulated that when anthrax occurs it has to be considered an act of terrorism."

Stunned, JC was silent for a moment before he gathered his thoughts and spoke.

"I saw one case of the cutaneous type that comes in thru a break in the skin when I was stationed overseas," he said. "It turned out that was one of the milder strains in a man who tanned animal hides for a living. It makes a real ugly spreading sore, solid black. Once you've seen one, you don't forget."

"I understand you have to inhale the germs to get the fatal kind that goes to your lungs and your lymph glands," Lauren said. "They said that the spores can hide for years until it gets in living tissue and then in a few days you're sick as a dog."

"That's right," JC said. "From what I remember, it sometimes starts with flu-like symptoms. If you catch it early, it can be cured with common antibiotics, but once the bacteria set up shop, which can be as early as three or four days, they start producing their toxins. By then, even if you kill the bacteria, the poisons continue to break down the cells of the body. It's almost always fatal from that stage and I don't think there's any real effective treatment yet."

He added, "There is one other kind that gets in your stomach if you ingest contaminated food, but that's really rare nowadays. You'd only really see it in a third world country."

She was attentive, "I didn't know about the cutaneous kind. These all look like the respiratory ones so far. They haven't been confirmed yet, and hopefully it'll turn out to be something else. The scientists are studying it right now, and, of course, the Feds will be in charge. They just wanted us to be aware.

"I don't think they know the source yet, like the cases at the post office, so there's nothing we can do now but wait and hope. Let's try to not let it spoil the rest of our evening," she said as she passed a slow moving car.

"Anyway, I haven't had much chance to follow the team this year. You think the ankle will hold up tonight?"

He was flattered. She had done some homework also, and she was better than he was when it came to leaving things back at the office. Lt. Long was full of pleasant surprises, more intriguing than his first chemistry set. He launched into the subject of basketball without giving what's-his-name Chandler or that other detective writer a second thought.

JC memorized her profile as she drove, and it didn't take him long. Pretty, smart and accomplished, she was able to guide them through phases one and two of "getting acquainted" with no significant injuries. By the time they approached the arena there was no more Dr. Thomas and Lt. Long, but just JC and Lauren out on a date, looking forward to having a good time at a basketball game.

She found a parking place. It might have been restricted, though he couldn't tell for sure in the dark. He liked the way she held his arm and guided him to the special security entrance on "F" street nearest "7th." She knew her way around, but let him lead anyway.

JC had never been to an event where his companion had to open her purse, show her credentials and actually check in a weapon with security, but Lauren was accustomed to the routine.

"Johnny," she said impishly with a wily smile. "I've just got to stop in the restroom for a second."

No one called Dr. Thomas that. Not in recent memory. In fact, only his mother ever addressed him that way. *How'd she know that's what his mother called him? That wouldn't even have been a part of his permanent record!*

"I'll wait in the concession line to ply you with Coke and popcorn."

Big smile, blue eyes twinkling again, "How could you know?"

The game had already started, and as JC waited in line, the noise from inside the arena was rhythmically deafening. There were a few other fans traipsing back and forth to the restrooms and some security people out in the concourse.

In addition to them, there was a sight that had become so common it was never noticed. Standing next to the wall was a janitor in a long sleeved uniform wearing a blue surgical mask out among the public during flu season. He was holding tightly to the long handle of his mop and pushing a four-wheeled rolling water bucket. The dark eyes darted here and there, nervously looking for a windmill to tilt. The name patch sewn over his shirt pocket contained only two letters. It read "Al."

Chapter Fifteen

After making their way to the seats just inside the first floor entry, twelve rows behind the team bench, they were soon caught up in the ball game. JC liked being out in the open crowd with the other mortals, not up on the higher private entrance levels with the corporate types. *Who knew what distracting business deals went on up there?*

Lauren admitted she was not a big sports fan, but between the loud music and the rowdy home crowd, it was impossible to not get excited. She was enjoying herself, and hopefully he would get credit for introducing her to some of the finer things in life.

During the intermission at half-time, they made their way out into the concourse and bumped into several acquaintances. The push of the crowd prevented anything but a hurried "Hello," and JC's friends were probably left wondering what floor of the hospital that pretty nurse worked.

She introduced him to a few people she knew as "JC Thomas," and he was pleased that she didn't attach much importance to the "Doctor" part. JC was proud that she had accepted a date with him, the person, not all of his old professors. The degree wasn't necessary. They were just two people together at a ball game.

By the time the second half started, he noticed that she was really caught up in the action. It was a five point back and forth game with superb athletes six to seven feet tall. They were fast and powerful, yet graceful. She joined in the cheering, and he was amazed at how much noise could come out of that small body.

The guard, who must be up to one hundred percent by now, made a steal, drove the length of the court, jumped from the free-throw line and slammed the ball through the hoop. Lauren squeezed his arm excitedly as if they had known each other forever, but then he noticed she also squeezed the arm of the guy on the other side whom she had never met. It was that kind of game!

The lead changed several times. It was tied with about three minutes to go and the shot clock running down when the shooting guard launched an off balance three point attempt. It was one of those extremely high, arcing shots that JC wished he'd never taken and it hung in the air forever. After a lifetime of silence from the twenty thousand onlookers, the net whispered, "Swish!" to the ear-splitting approval of the crowd, and JC was rewarded with an intimate bear hug that was meant for him only. Her twinkling blue eyes engulfed him and said every good thing he'd ever want to hear. The real world was a thousand miles away.

Unfortunately, the real world completed its round trip, as always, way too soon. The leading scorer fouled out on a terrible call by the official. Even the fans on the back rows could see that he hadn't touched the man he was guarding. They were both going for a loose ball. The swarthy man in the striped shirt with the whistle was from the west coast, had accepted a bribe and needed glasses. *Look at the replay.* But they never reverse a decision; the call stood and the guard had to leave the game. During the timeout while the coach considered who the replacement would be, Lauren's pager started to vibrate.

She read the message and he thought there might be a little mist in her eyes when she told him that suspicions had been confirmed. It was Anthrax. She needed to get back to the office for an urgent briefing. Was there any way he could catch a ride? She was so very sorry, and her whole body said so.

He was sorry too, but there were some things more important in life than a basketball game. He'd much rather be with her, especially now. He could see the final and highlights of a ball game any time.

As they approached the exit, he knew it would take a minute to retrieve her weapon and he excused himself to the men's room. He had matched her Coke for Coke.

The restroom was a huge mess. There was water all over the floor, there were no paper towels left, and people had tracked popcorn and trash in and out of the doorway. It was not an unusual state of affairs near the end of a big game with thousands of people, but this was as bad as he'd ever seen. It didn't look like the room had been cleaned since before the last game.

After finishing, JC wet his hands and reached for the soap, but when he pumped the dispenser, he was greeted with a spray in the face that made him blink. When he reached over for the adjacent dispenser he noticed a fine mist squirting out when he pressed it too. Looking closer he saw that the tip of the dispensers had been clogged up and small holes had been put in the tubes to direct the aerosol toward the user's face.

*Probably some teenage joke*, he thought. *Very funny -- Getting soap up the nose and in the face could hurt somebody.* Perturbed, he did what most people did: rinsed thoroughly, put his hands under the dryer that blew for a few seconds, and wiped them on his new blue blazer.

When he exited the restroom, the janitor was standing against the wall looking the other way. JC could see Lauren was still involved in the security lines, so he approached the man who really should be tending to the restroom and mopping the floor before someone slipped and fell. The soap dispensers needed fixing, and the paper towel dispensers needed to be restocked.

"Excuse me," JC said as the janitor started moving in the other direction.

*He probably doesn't understand English*, JC thought. It happened a lot in the ER, and with nobody around to translate he decided it was best to just demonstrate.

As he reached for the mop, the housekeeper grabbed the handle and jerked it away. The man held tightly to the mop which caused his arm to extend out beyond the shirt cuff, and that was when JC saw the huge black lesion on the back of the wrist.

It was as black as coal. Anthracite, the ancient Greek's word for coal, and the root word for the deadly bacteria. *My God! We had just been talking about it, and I've seen it once before. The man had cutaneous Anthrax!*

JC tried to take the poor fellow's arm and be of some help.

"You need to let someone look at—"

Suddenly the custodian pulled on the mop handle and a long knife came menacingly free of its sheath. For a brief instant the man looked JC in the eye. *Fight or flight time.* JC had seen many sharp tools, but not from this side.

The janitor decided. Instead of coming closer, he turned and ran toward the exit, toward the safety of the night. JC exercised the third reaction to stress: *fight, flight, or call for help.*

85

"Stop! Stop that man! He's got anthrax!"

There was never a cop around when needed, and that wasn't a cop the man was running toward now. That was a pretty, smart, young woman whom JC cared for in a brown sweater. She looked up at the commotion as he yelled "Anthrax" and at the man waving the long gleaming blade heading for the exit behind her.

Lauren wisely did not try to block his path, but stepped aside and bellowed, "Stop! Police! Stop or I'll shoot."

He did not. He dashed by her. Lauren reacted with discipline and reflex. The petite, angelic girl in the tan skirt with the perfect hair and the twinkling blue eyes, spread her two and a half inch heels, slightly bent her knees, aimed her weapon and squeezed the trigger.

She hit him one inch to the right of his left shoulder blade. The janitor screamed and jerked violently. The knife clattered to the concrete and the man's body crumpled to the floor.

From somewhere deep inside the arena, an irritatingly loud buzzer sounded.

Chapter Sixteen

Dr. John Christopher Thomas was a very calm surgeon. Whether he came by it naturally, or it was the result of countless all-nighters he'd spent fighting misery and death in unbelievably broken bodies, he didn't know. When people were bleeding and screaming or throwing up their hands and passing out, he was always in control. He was the one they depended on in a crisis: the captain of the ship, et cetera. But this wasn't an operating room, and this wasn't a ship.

This was some wild-eyed assassin with a long knife and a deadly third world disease threatening to kill him and Lauren. This was terror in a crowd of innocent bystanders and dramatic police action to stop it. This was beyond his ability to readily understand. Things like this didn't happen to him. They involved other people, and then he just saw it on the news or cleaned up its effects in the ER.

When the assailant's body fell, some unseen finger pushed JC's "Slow playback" button. The world began to come to him one mute disjointed frame at a time. He played a role as a part of the scene; real life had abruptly departed for the second time that night. Now some replacement existence dangerously threatened to substitute for reality.

Through the haze in the concourse, he saw the custodian and the knife lying on the dirty concrete floor surrounded by security guards. He saw Lauren standing in their midst with her weapon drawn. In another frame, he could see that she was unhurt and looking his way. The pictures slowly began to come closer together, and after a few more frames, he felt himself being firmly escorted down the hall in the other direction. JC fastened his mental seatbelt without being instructed.

His escorts appropriated one of the concession areas, where they stationed him out of the main thoroughfare. He could still see the activity, though. Soon his adrenal glands returned from their short break. He couldn't see Lauren from where he stood, but he knew she was okay. In fact, she was better than okay. The lady could obviously take care of herself, and him, and a whole lot of other people, too.

The steel mesh barriers at the entrances to the concourse rumbled down like thunder from above. They clanged to the floor, locking in place so that nobody could leave the arena. The first responders and the building's security force promptly summoned their brothers in arms who rapidly gathered from the nearby streets and filled the outer halls.

In the next fifteen to twenty minutes, SWAT teams swarmed in wearing helmets, goggles and heavy body armor. Crews in hazmat gear with tinted hoods from outer space and roving gangs of blue jackets labeled "FBI" or "ATF" joined in while yelling into their microphones. There were more black figures with headgear and earpieces than you'd find on game day in Oakland and more turmoil than in the climax of a bad science fiction movie.

*Strange*, JC thought, *there were few civilians in the halls or lining up behind the metal curtains trying to get out.* Sometime later he learned that the buzzer that had sounded when the man fell signaled only the beginning of overtime. Tied at the end of regulation play, the extra five-minute period commenced. The chaos in the outer passageway remained unknown to the crowd. Waiting for the time extension to begin they had stayed glued to their seats in the cavernous arena. The roar of the crowd and time buzzer during regular play had masked the sound of Lauren's gunfire.

Almost no one left early. Most of the twenty thousand fans remained in their seats at the end of the overtime when the public address began to broadcast the carefully worded script:

"Ladies and gentleman, could I have your attention, please. A small, isolated incident just occurred in the concourse, but the threat has been resolved. I repeat: you are not in danger at this time. The situation has been contained. However, as a matter of precaution, it will be several minutes before the area can be reopened to the public. Please remain in your seats and we will keep you informed. Again, there is no immediate danger. Thank you for your cooperation."

Whether it was the familiar voice of the home team announcer or the presence of an official at the entrance of each section, the crowd collectively gasped, but was generally well contained. Every party had access to at least one cell phone, of course, and these were activated in unison to apprise friends on the outside of the situation. The abundance of outgoing calls, texts, and multimedia messages temporarily overwhelmed the tower, which did not get used by the rescuers. They had a separate contained communication system.

As with any large crowd, there were those present who grumbled, those who sat back down and began to fan themselves, and those who emptied their bottles of water before realizing that all of the restrooms were located out in the concourse. Some of the observers, by virtue of their net worth or the number of votes they received in the last election, immediately became more important than their neighbors. Their excuses to leave were far more compelling, but since anthrax was not a respecter of capitalism nor democracy, they were politely restricted to their areas just like all the other fans. The only exceptions were a few reporters, present in large numbers for the critical ball game, who managed to leak out and steal a few pictures of the concourse.

This was Washington, D.C., the nation's capital. Officials

here had planned ahead and were well prepared and organized for rapid initial response to a crisis situation. The people here were accustomed to large important events. But, this was Washington, D.C., the nation's capital. The complex processing procedures and details would take at least all night.

JC and Lauren had been hustled off to separate dressing rooms for decontamination and debriefing. Since they were both in the high-risk group for exposure, having been in the restrooms, all possible precautions were taken. They each had a shower with disinfectant for the hair, face and body and were given clean white barrier coveralls to wear. All of their possibly contaminated clothes, including the new blazer, the knee-length tan skirt, the sweater and underwear were confiscated and burned.

After nearly two hours, they were escorted separately through the narrow back passageways and restricted elevators to be reunited on the third floor in the team management's suite of private offices.

This time trivial greetings did not come to mind and no Coke can interfered. They had shared a tumultuous, threatening event and became vastly closer because of it. She was a beautiful sight. Stunning in a white jumpsuit, as they approached each other, she flashed that same wily smile and inquired, "Do you need a hug?" She, then, opened her arms to offer a long intimate embrace. To a surgeon, the familiar faint scent of disinfectant in her hair was a comforting perfume as their faces stayed together for a long time. Through the thin paper coveralls, JC thought he felt her trembling a bit, but it just as easily could have been him.

After a moment of reflection, which can sometimes change a person's life, she jokingly started, "John, thank God you're alright. I really haven't been on a serious date in a long time and if it ended with you dying, what would that say as me as a professional?" Then she solemnly continued, "Seriously, that man could have killed you. It's always a wonder when no 'innocents' get injured with so many people around. Amazing with someone that crazed that no one was stabbed. It's hard to keep my anger in check when someone does that in a place like this. There were kids in there ... "

Before JC could respond, the door to the suite opened; a

man with an earpiece entered. He was an impressive figure in his blue jacket and tie with a slight limp from some previous experience. Before he opened his mouth, it was obvious who was in charge. The two lesser figures with him had badges, foreboding side arms and large phones, but their presence was barely noteworthy.

The one in command began to speak as he looked straight into their eyes.

"Lt. Long, Dr. Thomas, I'm Pat, FBI counterterrorism."

It was implied, and therefore, not necessary to say, *I'm a soldier who's been there, not a politician. This is serious. I'm running the show, and if I ever had a last name, it's not important to share that information at this time.*

While he spoke in a firm, calm voice, it was obvious that this was not the lead-in for a dialogue.

"Lt. Long, your Chief of Police and The Mayor send their congratulations. Thanks to you and your quick reaction, you and Dr. Thomas have helped save a number of our fellow citizens tonight."

Pat continued without pause, "There are some things we need to talk about. No one else needs to know *what we talk about.* I have thoroughly studied both of your personal histories. Lt. Long your current position with D.C. Metro and Dr. Thomas your previous military experience comfort me in sharing information with you."

JC thought, *this didn't seem like a man who needed to be comforted, he was just being nice.*

Pat's voice immediately snapped JC back to attention, "First, the soap dispensers and the hand dryers in several of the restrooms, both men's and women's, were altered to deliver an aerosol spray toward the face of the user. We have to assume this was accomplished six or seven days ago, prior to the last event here. Ultraviolet indicates that spores were swarming in large concentrations, and a number of people, you two included, have been exposed. We know this is Anthrax. The particular strain has yet to be identified, but with a terror attack, we must take all precautions.

"Second, we're going to have to isolate a number of people

for a while. We know that human-to-human transmission is extremely rare, but we really can't take any chances. Lieutenant, since you are current on your immunizations given to law enforcement by D.C. Metro, you'll be at lower risk. Dr. Thomas, the shots you had while on active duty might still offer some protection, but we're going to get both of you started on antibiotics.

"From the information I have,"—*and he had a lot*, JC thought. *Neither of them had mentioned their vaccines* —"we're concerned that a number of people were exposed six days ago at the last event, in addition to this evening. Teams are working now to identify and trace those people for medical evaluation.

"Third, Lt. Long, the fact that you were diligent enough to bring the suspect down with a well-placed shot in the middle of a crowd of innocents before he escaped is a God-send. We have him secured and basically uninjured. We will be able to obtain some useful information."

*To a man like Pat,* surmised JC, *the small whole in the man's back from a single bullet that didn't pierce any vital organs qualified as basically uninjured.*

Pat concluded, "We'll be in touch, and a very personal "Well Done" for your service from your fellow citizens tonight."

Pat left to the tune of "The Star Spangled Banner" without waiting for a reply. He was a very busy man. JC was proud to be on his side.

The Chief of Police, whom JC recognized from his picture, had entered the room unnoticed and now he spoke. "Great job, Lauren. You and your boyfriend have done a tremendous service tonight. Unfortunately, a lot of people will soon know who you are and the reporters will be lining up. You might want to try and avoid the public eye until we can get things under control. Dr. Thomas, I don't believe the reporters know your identity and I don't see why you can't take the antibiotic pack and go on home where you can get some rest under voluntary isolation for now. Be sure to contact Lt. Long if you have any problems."

"Thank you," JC said. "Sounds like a good idea, but, uh... I guess we came in Lauren's car tonight."

"Well, I'm going to need her for a while. The paper work just won't go away. Why don't you take her vehicle for now? You two can switch rides sometime in the next few days."

"Oh, almost forgot. It's pretty cold out there, Pat wanted me to give you his jacket."

It was a perfect fit: blue with the letters FBI on the back.

"You know," Lauren said. "Right now, that paperwork might be a good distraction."

She turned those big blue eyes to JC again and handed him her keys. His battlefield promotion to "Boyfriend" by the Chief of Police had not gone unnoticed by either of them.

"I'll give you a call tomorrow. I've got your number."

She knew he knew what she meant; the twinkle had returned.

JC drove Lauren's black Ford Crown Victoria straight home, reflecting on the dramatic events. He was hesitant to stop. Pat was probably watching. Plus, the big desk sergeant had been looking for him since midnight.

Chapter Seventeen

While government officials and lobbyists were scattered throughout the District enjoying their Sunday brunch and deciding how best to deflect and whom to blame for this most recent attack, a diverse group of people who were always on call had gathered. Their meeting took place several blocks away from the downtown arena in a windowless conference room inside a fortified building that no longer offered public tours.

Communication barriers between the various security agencies over the years led to a rather unhealthy competition for funding. Or was it the other way around? After 9/11, it became obvious that organizational changes had to be made. Pat was laboring under the most recent and more effective guidelines of the Department of Homeland Security, but the system was still far from perfect. Secret plays were difficult when the other team was in your huddle.

One of the tools he had found useful was to assemble a special group of advisors, an unofficial "kitchen cabinet." The most effective way to get the job done required people without a desire for public credit. Pat included four people from the CIA,

ATF and NSA. Other people, whose positions had never been advertised under equal opportunities employment law attended. Anyone who had been or ever would be a consultant for a major news organization he automatically disqualified from participation.

Pat personally selected each of these individuals. They were not elected nor politically appointed. They were brilliant, open-minded problem solvers. They loved their country and represented the best and the brightest. Every bit of their work fell under one of the nine exemptions and was not subject to the Freedom of Information Act.

Pat gave the group a concise account of what was known about the attack. He stressed the fact that all information corroborated that the man detained would be the one who knew the most about the attack at the arena. After listing the various eye-witnesses, arena employee files and arena employee testimonies—including the female that had surprised Al on an earlier occasion. Pat opened the floor for discussion.

One of the group members, a grandmother of three, who currently demonstrated her vivid imagination in her work as a mystery novel writer spoke. She had a considerable gift with words.

"Patrick, anything new from the Army out at Ft. Anthrax, Maryland, as to which little bacterial boogers we're dealing with this time?"

Pat paused. Anyone who didn't know better would think this woman cumbersome to getting at the truth. The facts that she was both a genius and had saved millions of Americans lives in the past were known to few people.

He responded, "Not yet. They're still unwinding the DNA to determine the specific strain before they can start to track its origin."

"Speaking of strains," said one of the others not paid to be a 'yes-man', "Detrick's strainer has been pretty porous of late. Seems like they've let some pretty big chunks get through the screen. Hope they've got that fixed."

"They're the absolute best in the free world at knowing the bio-terror-defense business," replied the grandmother. "But, if you get enough flesh-eating men working around enough man-eating plants you're gonna' have a problem from time to time."

"Probably spent all their resources trying to comply with OSHA, also, can you imagine how many HIPPA regs they're under?", the man rationalized.

"Hard to keep up with the other side who can skip the white mice and monkey stage and go directly to clinical trials on humans. Cold war's been in the freezer for a long time, but I hear they just got a new microwave," said one of the others. This gruff, robust man was a Colonel previously. Technically now "unemployed" he, ironically, did more work for the government than most people in Washington.

Pat called the group back to task. 9/11 had shown him the merit of imagination and the free flow of ideas, but organization was still the key to fighting and winning the new war. It was his job to consider all the possibilities, to leave nothing out, and then deselect until he got close to the truth before making a plan of action.

One of the other men with a specific interest in history took up, "Looks to me, Pat, that you've got a bit of a dilemma with your prisoner."

"How's that, Daniel?"

"This man we're holding is obviously not working alone and there could easily be other devices out there filled with spores and already in place. We all remember they got four planes off the ground last time, not just one. Given enough time in the tank, he'll see things our way, but we need what he knows pretty damn quick.

"If you go straight to the rubber hose, a judge might turn him loose later and you might have to give up some secrets in court that could hurt us, like in the past. On the other hand, we can't afford to have another 30,000 of our people exposed."

"I understand what you're saying," Pat said, "but I don't see the dilemma. There's only one clear choice. We've got to know and we've got to know now. We've been working on him since midnight and the hose is still in the closet."

"Whatever you think, Pat, go ahead. I'll be a good character witness at your trial." Daniel remarked with sincerity.

"Just don't let 'em take my pension."

Pat had not been selected for his job by avoiding personal

risks. He was in the business to protect the American people, and he was good at it.

"We've all got a lot to think about ... why don't we reassemble here in twelve hours for progress reports."

*******************

Miles from Washington there is an undisclosed area that has no ZIP code. This region does not appear on any map and has yet to be discovered by Wal-Mart. There is only one property in this neighborhood and it is an exclusive hotel with no New Testaments in the bedside stands. In fact, there are no bedside stands. The resort has never been rated by any of the travel guide services, but if it were, it would warrant fifty stars and thirteen stripes. Pat's group holds the controlling sole interest in this property, and this is where the custodian known as Al was taken. He was accommodated in a small barren room with all the benefits of the significantly Modified American Plan.

Several things about him were quickly discovered:

His real first name was Ali, and he had come to this country an unwelcome visitor some two to three years earlier. He was not one of the "We the People" crowd that had pledged to ensure domestic tranquility. He was not capable of planning this degree of terror attack on his own. He was a puppet, and once the wires were cut it would not be long before he would collapse to the floor. Unfortunately, the ones who held his strings must have realized this and prepared other puppets.

His initial medical exam was quite thorough and was performed by a female physician. It revealed a significant cutaneous lesion of anthrax on his wrist, though he showed no signs of pulmonary involvement from the deadly organism. The temperature, chills, and malaise that he experienced were due to the influenza virus that was so prevalent in the community at the time. It was not deemed necessary to fully inform him of these findings. Complete disclosure was not included in the particular Modified American Plan he had chosen.

The plan did provide unlimited food, drink, and medicine, but most of the previous guests were suspicious. They expressed concerns to the management that these necessities may have been altered in some way and, like Ali, initially refused all of these amenities.

The heating and air in the building worked extremely well for the purposes for which they had been designed. The environment could subtly cycle, a degree at a time, from 45 to 95 degrees Fahrenheit. The humidity could range from nosebleed dry to salty sweat running down and burning your eyes. The guests were not aware of the gradual room temperature changes, and in this individual's case, the conditions aggravated the influenza, which in itself was producing fever and fluid loss followed by bed-shaking chills.

The sleeping conditions here were reminiscent of the Intensive Care Unit. He was routinely awakened as soon as he tried to drift off and then probed and questioned while monitors beeped and blinked continuously. The bed bent in the middle and was so uncomfortable that every one of his joints ached and every muscle threatened to cramp if he moved the wrong way. In the unlikely event that he did become accustomed to the incessant, unrelenting beeping, it suddenly and inexplicably stopped, only to be replaced by a moment of absolute silence followed by the squeal of an unanswered alarm.

Like bad waiters, the attendants only came when he didn't want them. They were constantly asking questions and offering advice, though not necessarily good advice. There were four people who came in pairs to question him. Two were especially threatening and abrasive. One woman wore a star with six points around her neck and showed no respect for men at all. Another man was loud and gruff, with a permanent, visible tattoo that read "USMC". He constantly played with a stout leather dog leash. These were just the types that Ali had been trained to resist in the camps.

The prisoner did have some support, however, from two other people who were fluent in his native language. One of these was a comforting nurse who was very young and very pretty and whose uniform did not quite cover her knees. She kept her head modestly bowed in his presence, but when she came close and knelt to tend his wound he could smell the lavender fragrance that issued from her neck.

The second ally was introduced to the man as Hussein, a devout cleric with a full beard, who, like some other religious leaders, occasionally manipulated the truth. He brought with him a copy of the Quran and read selected portions aloud as had been intended by The Prophet many centuries ago. The reading was almost singing and was of great comfort to the prisoner. He could depend on this man for spiritual counseling. Hussein was known to those in charge of the facility as Captain David Sanchez, previously a linebacker from an Academy in Colorado who had learned the detainee's language and customs while stationed in country. Capt. Sanchez had been fortunate to find a last minute substitute for his usual Sunday task, chasing the toddlers in the nursery. He was Methodist.

Ali found that he was able, by stretching to his full height and standing on tip-toe, to see an opaque skylight outside his cell in the hall. By this clever method, he was able to deduce the passage of time. Light vs. dark, which was very important to one who is isolated. He was unaware that, due to a design flaw in the hotel's illumination system, the daylight here lasted only three hours while the nights were a full four.

His two friends told him they just couldn't understand why the leaders of his group had not offered him inoculations to prevent his contracting anthrax. The vaccine could be obtained at any drug store. They did not bother to clarify the fact that the skin lesions of anthrax virtually never progressed to the fatal pulmonary disease, and he had no way to reference the reality of what he was told.

With the lack of sleep, lack of fluid, miserable fever and sweats followed by chilling cold and muscle cramps, the lesion on his wrist quickly became more irritated. It was growing and his whole arm now felt painful and swollen. Through the slough of the overlying skin, he could start to see the tendon cords move back and forth with each effort of clinching his fist.

Ali calculated that at least three days had passed since his capture. He had told his tormentors nothing, and he had bought valuable time for the others in his group. He was miserable. He feared that his whole body would be taken over with the rot on his arm and he would die in a slow painful manner if he were not treated soon.

The first step in his conversion was like the taming of any wild beast. He began to drink the water they provided. He took small sips at first, but then gratefully gulped a second bottle. The man had been allowing, in fact requesting, frequent dressing changes and salve on his wrist by the tender hand of the nurse, but he knew this was not helping. His two friends convinced him that he would require surgery to clean the sore and keep it from spreading.

Ali knew that he would need an anesthetic for the painful surgery, but he did not want to be unconscious. He was offered the choice of staying awake with a numbing block to his arm for the operation. The doctor even offered to give a demonstration of the electrical nerve stimulator, which would be used to define the exact spot to place the deadening medicine. However, having once felt and survived a 50,000 volt Taser on his back, and with some prompting from his attendants, he was left to imagine what the electricity might feel like on the more sensitive parts of his body.

He was so miserable that he finally chose to be put to sleep with a general anesthetic for the procedure. There was a variety of sedative and hypnotic medications which had been evaluated at similar facilities around the world. One of these medications induced a hypnotic trance much like a super truth serum, and this was felt to be the drug of choice. This particular compound had not been evaluated, much less approved, by the food and drug administration. In this case, though, it was deemed appropriate. The compound was thought to have no long-term side effects and left no memory of the event. The patient was taken into a small operating room, an IV was started in his other arm, and the medicine was injected. Ali held the cool, soft hand of the pretty nurse who would see after his physical needs, while his religious advisor, the cleric Hussein, was present to watch over his soul.

As the man drifted into conscious sedation, before the surgeon started cutting away the dead tissue from his wound, they were all amazed at how much the patient enjoyed talking in his sleep.

*******************

98

In spite of the frantic activity precipitated by the terror attack at the stadium, the Chief, LB and Tim were left to work on their multiple murder cases. Huddled on the third floor of the district headquarters, they were engaged in the grinding detail needed to catch a killer. Time, they knew, was not on their side. Most people would not spend their Sundays at work but for these people the day on the calendar made no difference.

"We're pretty sure about the identity of the second one we found," LB said. "Barbara Jefferson. She was a lobbyist from the Midwest who split her time between Washington and home. It was not uncommon for her to be away on extended junkets, explaining why it was a week before she was reported missing."

Tim broke in, "She was so mutilated it wasn't possible for her sister to be a hundred percent sure from a photo, but we're pretty sure this is our Jane Doe Number Two. DNA confirmation is going to take some time, especially with all that's going on now, and we still can't find dental records on her. We don't have a local address on her yet, but we'll get that pretty soon. Then we can start to follow her footsteps just before she was killed. The sister thought she might have had her dental implants done overseas, but she's not sure. I don't think the sister and her were that close."

"I still don't understand," LB wondered aloud. "He took the breasts in all three of our victims, but left the fingerprints and teeth in the first one. Either he didn't have time to finish his work or he didn't care if we ID'd her pretty quickly. He went to the trouble to remove the fingerprints in the next two, but left the teeth in the second one."

"Yeah," Tim interrupted, "but we couldn't find a dentist who worked on Number Two."

"That's the point," she continued. "If her dental work was done overseas, it would take us a long time to make a match, and we might not ever get that information."

"This third girl had teeth and fingerprints removed," Chief Lane said. "No way to know her identity, but that peculiar sun tan... I don't think she got that around here. Possibly Two and Three had been out of the country, and if they were together, could that be our connection?"

"You're forgetting the first one had never left the US," Tim said. "Didn't even have a passport."

The Chief had not forgotten. "Could be a ploy to throw us off—waste our time on a red herring, but we still need to look for any tie they might have had. Tim, why don't you talk to that sister again and let's see if we can get Number Two's passport record. Might come in handy later."

"Sure will, Chief," Tim said. "I'm still thinking these were just random targets for this psycho, but if there's a connection, I'll find it."

"You know," the Chief said. "This guy might be both crazy and smart, but like LB said, you have to be persistent. We're about to learn who these flowers were, but we've got to keep digging until we get rid of all the weeds. There are a lot more flowers out there to protect until they're ready to bloom."

Chapter Eighteen

Basil crouched on the floor seething with disgust and anger in the basement of his flat. He had walked to the small store very early for a newspaper to delight himself with the photographs from the attack, to revel in the first fruits of their mission so long in the ripening. The goal of his small cell was to create terror and uncertainty and death among the Americans.

With the blessing of Allah they would bring this country to its knees. Israel would be toothless and Jerusalem would be purged of its evil. The more people killed and mutilated in the most unsuspecting and horrible fashion, the more disruption and panic were achieved. The bar had been set very high on the 11th of September, and Basil had expected even more significant results and continuing mayhem from this attack at the stadium. They did damage, true enough, but he sought to set a new standard. They would cause many more deaths with the next part of the plan.

Now he knew, and it had been proven for all to see: the custodian was a coward. He was useful only because of his placement at the arena many months ago, but the leaders must have suspected his weakness. They kept him on the outside and unaware of the many details of the master plan.

The custodian did not know Basil and had never seen him. His only contact was with the currier, Kafeel, but Basil observed Ali many times from a safe distance. Over the months he spent in Washington, he watched this one become weaker and give in to the temptations of the infidels. He was soft and rotting inside. He was not mujahedeen. He would not be blessed in Paradise.

When the Sheik summoned the members of the cell to gather in the city of Las Vegas shortly after his arrival in this country, they were kept apart for testing. That was when Basil had become suspicious of the captured one. He observed the man there in the American desert and watched him drink alcohol. Basil saw him participate in the indulgences of the infidels. He gave in to the sin that was abundant in that place. He saw him with the painted women, the haughty ones who did not cover themselves. They all knew from that time, but he was necessary. He would be used.

The man, Ali, should have slashed to death the one who exposed him before the alarm could be raised. He then should have cut out his own heart before the crowd. The throng of Americans would have seen the blood of a true martyr and come to know the passion of their enemy. They would have run in panic out of the building and been scattered into the city without knowing of the fatal spores they carried. Many more would have been infected and many more would have died from the deadly disease before the weapons were discovered. Their fear and dread would have been enormous.

But now the man who called himself Al was captured and would give up any secrets he possessed at the first hint of torture and pain. He was forever shamed, having been brought down by this small weak infidel, a lowly woman, nonetheless, who did not know her rightful place. Hopefully, he would die soon at the hands of the Americans. He could give dangerous information and increase the attention, but he could not expose Basil. The leaders far away were indeed very smart men, guided by their devotion to The Prophet.

The city and the whole country were in some degree of chaos--off balance--unsteady from the shock. The great Satan would use tens, perhaps hundreds, of millions of dollars in resources and man power to find and save the infected ones among them. They should not waste the money and disrupt their market places for these few lives, but they would. They would even work to save a useless child from dying. That was one of their many weaknesses.

At least one of their congressmen was known to be infected and many other government officials were exposed. It was possible that some of Basil's countrymen were present in the crowd or among the workers at the arena. There were always unseen consequences from a direct terror attack, but if a few of the faithful should perish, Allah would forgive. There was always "collateral damage" as the Americans would say.

The loss of infidel lives was of no consequence to Basil. Like the first woman he had butchered here in the city, she was of no further use to him. She served only as a ruse to throw the police off his track. He would kill many others, if he desired, to confuse them until his work was done.

A small stone had again been tossed into a quiet pool. This could be stirred into a large wave, but it was time now to gather a much bigger rock, one that would engulf the whole shore. There were many targets and he had decided how to move next.

It was twilight as he stretched out at prayer time. He, then, dressed himself and placed the contact lenses with care. His eyes were much less irritated now, and even though he would be working in the dark, he vowed to always use the brown tint. Basil was almost invisible besides the necessary waterproof pack which contained his protective clothing as he moved through the darkened streets.

He carried no metal weapons to alert the detectors but still carefully avoided certain busy areas of the district. The arena was being used to hold some of those exposed to the anthrax. The cleanup required many laborers and many of the press were present with their cameras.

The city had greatly increased numbers of police cars prowling through the concrete canyons, but Basil knew the isolated passageways and could move about on foot with ease. He was just an innocent resident out for a walk on a Sunday evening. After an hour of travel, he approached his next target's home.

Basil approached the small screen porch at the back of the

102

subject's residence. He gained entrance with no problem for a man of his skills. After putting on his gloves, surgical coveralls, shoe covers, mask and cap he went inside. Not one hair was exposed.

The weakened and debilitated man lay sleeping in his bed. The hunter's approach awakened him. Startled by the sudden appearance of this ghostly figure in his room, he jerked upright and his mouth immediately opened to make a sound. He posed no threat to the assassin and could not even command his voice to cry out in terror. The powerful killer struck quickly and pounced on top of the animal before a sound could be uttered. He held a pillow tightly over his prey's face, quickly smothering the victim whose flailing arms could do no damage. The victim saw no trace of Basil under his cover, only a ghostly image. The foolish American known as Charles O'Reilly had breathed his last.

In the kitchen, the reaper selected from a variety of the man's cutlery. Sometime he would try the electric knife, but not tonight. The eight-inch blade he chose was very sharp. Basil the butcher deftly harvested his prize from the near bloodless field.

He then prepared the room for the fire he had planned. He would have plenty of time to escape undetected before anyone noticed the blaze. It would be much later, if ever, before it could be discovered that this man had not simply fallen into a drug-induced coma from the influence of pain medication while smoking in his bed.

As the assassin was cleaning the tools, removing evidence and packing to leave, the sound of loud voices approached the front entrance.

"Hey, Charlie, wake up ... we brought you some rations."

The intruders must have had a key, because the door suddenly opened and two men entered with sacks of food and bottles of alcohol to drink. The adept killer, a man of cat-like reflex, seized the butchering knife. The first visitor had no warning before the blade entered his heart and his knees buckled. Bright red blood erupted through the air and fell all over the rug and floor. There was so much that it would have soiled Basil's garments had he not been so quick to move.

The second man weakly put his arms in front of his face before Basil landed a powerful kick. The man's forearm broke in a grotesque fashion as he received a glancing blow to his head. The killer immediately delivered such a violent twist to the neck that he wondered if the cracking noise might have been heard outside.

He threw the body to the ground and prepared for another foe, but only two of the herd had stumbled in and spoiled his plan. No other people knew of the events at Charlie O'Reilly's.

Basil was mujahedeen, a holy warrior selected because he was a psychopathic killer. If he had ever possessed the emotion to be frightened, he had lost that long ago. There was no panic, just calm consideration of the circumstance. *Might there be more people coming? Would these two be missed soon?*

The savagery in the room could not be concealed now, and the law officers would not be fooled once three bodies were discovered. He must adapt his plan. There was time for him to quickly collect one other piece tonight and then move his hunting ground into a different region.

The coverings and gloves had spared any stain to the killer's clothes and they were removed outside the back door. Placing all the items he had touched and the part he had murdered for in the backpack with the cleaned knife, he left the house and moved through the streets for a safe distance before hailing a taxi. The hunter seldom used a public cab. He did not like the close contact, but there was urgency now. His scent might be discovered at any time and he must collect another trophy before the night ended.

Basil kept his face from view but his hand demonstrated a large amount of money when he gave the driver an address for a convenience store located some distance away, near the beltway on Ridgeview Avenue. There was no word spoken during the ride. The maps he had studied were accurate. They would pass by Dr. Thomas's home a few blocks before arriving at the convenience store.

As the cab approached the house, Basil was taken aback once more. There was a black Ford Crown Victoria with an official license plate parked in Dr. Thomas's driveway. How could that be at this time of night? Many lights inside were on. He recognized the style of car as one belonging to the police of this district. He had not expected to see the police at this house.

Furious, he masked his outrage so that the cabbie would not notice. Basil knew he must change his plan, again. He could not afford to kill a police officer at this point. Learning from 9/11, to kill certain people, even in this country, brought more intense scrutiny. The killing of any law enforcement would greatly rally resources to his own hunt; a fact that wouldn't matter later but for now, he must avoid. He had not found the prize at the man's office and now he would have to wait once more.

The butcher collected himself and exited the car at the convenience store with his belongings. He gave the driver a reasonable, but not excessive, tip. He had one trophy for the night and decided it would be best to not risk exposure. The doctor had been up and about, and the police had been there in his home. He would disappear for now and save this one for another time.

The cab driver pulled away musing, *That's a hell of a long way to go for a pack of cigarettes at this time of night.* But no matter, he had driven the streets of the nation's capital for fifteen years. During his time, he had known many people in Washington to go a lot farther and spend a lot more to get a lot less.

******************

JC did not notice the vacant taxi retracing its route outside his home. He was much too engrossed on the phone with Lauren. The strong magnetism between JC and Lauren made perfect sense. Like electrons and protons, they contained the same core material but it emitted in very different ways—ways that remained unfilled without the other to balance it. Neither of them had anyone else in the picture to shield and dilute the attraction. Finally, the close proximity both physically and emotionally forced by the dramatic events the night before solidified the bond. They had fallen that fast, that hard and they both knew it.

Lauren had been up all night, except for a brief nap, when her brother called from Heathrow. He had been following the anthrax story on the net when he saw his baby sister's face halfway around the world.

JC joked, "Great shot of you on the front page. I downloaded it for my wallpaper."

105

"John! Is it the one where I'm blowing the smoke off my gun or the one with my hair in my face trying to block the camera?"

"Well, now it's the one with the big orange icon covering your nose. Could you maybe bring the other ones out tomorrow after you have a chance to rest? I'd like to make copies."

"No. But, I need to escape from my sudden press following. How 'bout I bring your car back right after lunch, instead?"

"Yeah. You sure it's no bother? I'm planning to stay in another few days until my nasal swabs are negative. I don't want to expose you to any risks."

"I'm sure you're safe, and don't forget, I know a doctor. Also, I've been vaccinated against you…or, against the anthrax spores your carrying. I don't know if they make a vaccine against you." She laughed, "You need anything else?"

"Maybe bring a pizza?"

"I exist for pizza. Plain pepperoni for me, but if you want some other topping, I could make do."

"No, that'd be great. I used to like mushrooms, but I'm trying to stay away from anything that can form spores for a while."

"Can't wait ... see you early afternoon."

"Lauren, you're a lifesaver you know."

JC would never know how right he was about her and her black Ford that stood guard outside in his driveway.


Chapter Nineteen

The counter-terror group assembled at 2 a.m. The prisoner had been held for some twenty-six hours by then, and Pat reported what they had learned. It took the better part of two minutes.

One of the group members then asked, "How much longer can we afford to keep the hose in the closet and the board out of the water, Pat?"

"Our people out there at the lodge feel that if we tried more extreme measures, this one would just make up stuff that he thought we wanted to hear. There's no way to confirm anything he'd say without a second source, and we don't have that yet."

Pat continued, "These radical leaders read and watch more news than all of us put together. They're training their robots how to react to the interrogation measures that they think we use. Fortunately for us, you can't believe anything you see in the newspapers anymore. We expect to have everything he knows by 15:30 hours today. I'd say we huddle again then."

"Patrick, aren't you cutting the deadline a little thin?" another of the group asked.

"Yeah, you're probably right. Let's say 16:00 to be on the safe side."

******************

By the middle of a cold Monday morning, a van from Community Services was winding through the streets of the district looking for a particular address. The two home health nurses inside were approaching the house of their third patient of the day. In spite of the chaotic crisis conditions all around, their medical care continued to be needed by the sick and infirm.

The previous stops had been easy follow-up visits. The first was a woman with recent knee replacement surgery who was doing well. She could straighten her leg and raise it from the bed ten times and she could also bend her knee to a right angle. The metal staples that had held her skin together had been removed three days before and her incision was healing with no problems. She was near independent and almost ready to be discharged from home care.

The second patient had been an overweight man with an ulcer on his foot from diabetes mellitus. The two nurses had been treating him for over a month and he was slowly improving in spite of a fondness for chocolate Oreos dunked in low-calorie Slimfast. He was properly scolded, his sugar level was recorded, and his wound was cleaned and dressed. It was just a routine start to the long workweek.

Judy was at the wheel as the van crept up to the address of their new client. She had been an army nurse for four years and spent time in the ER before working a cardiac floor. Brad, who had just received his five-year pin, was reading the patient's notes from the hospital.

"This man is aged fifty-four. Dr. Thomas revised a right total hip replacement on him last week for a fracture of his femur around the metal stem. He was in good shape when he left the hospital on Friday. Looks like he'd had his other hip replaced a couple 'a months ago."

"He's only fifty-four and he's already had both hips replaced and one of them revised?"

"Yup, doesn't seem fair, does it?"

"Some people have a lot of bad luck I guess," Judy said. "Anything else going on?"

"No, says he'd been in good health," Brad responded, "Maybe does a little extra drinking. Works full time as an estate planner."

"Okay, then we'll want to check his vitals and help him with some activities of daily living. He should be a pro with hip surgery by now."

"I'd guess so. I'll change his dressing and assess his incision and we'll be done in time to grab some lunch."

"Yeah, sounds good to me," Judy said. "I'm starving."

"You try that new Mexican place out here?"

"No, but I've heard it's good. Might be just the thing on a cold day like today."

They were experienced nurses. Between them they'd seen almost everything, and they felt well prepared for their new patient visit. The two were a little concerned when no one answered their knock or responded to their "Hello, Home Health." The front door was unlocked so they let themselves in and promptly forgot about their lunch plans.

No amount of preparation could have made the sight less startling--*Three corpses and blood everywhere!* There was a body near the front door with a grotesque appearance. The neck was twisted so that the head was almost facing backward, and his forearm was bent double with the bones sticking out through the skin. Just a few yards away lay a second man, dead eyes still open, with a massive amount of dried blood soaking his shirt and the surrounding rug and floor.

They could see in the bedroom beyond, where there was

108

another body clad only in a pajama top. His leg was folded across his trunk in an impossible position for someone with a normal hip. A wound of some eight to ten inches in length gaped along the side of his left upper thigh, but surprisingly little blood was on the sheet.

Judy's knees buckled. It was worse than the memories of her ER rotation, but she managed to recover before falling. She was able to collect herself enough to catch Brad and lead him back out the front door where they both sank down on the front steps and dialed 911 for help.

By the time the siren approached and stopped, Judy and Brad were still in some degree of shock, sitting on the doorstep as the two uniformed officers approached. They just pointed through the open door where the police could see part of the horror that lay inside.

One of the patrolmen exclaimed, "Oh my God! They said there were three bodies but we weren't expecting anything like this. Was anyone else here aside from you two?"

"I don't think so," Judy said. "We saw the bodies as soon as we went inside. I was afraid I was going to pass out, so we came back out here to sit down and wait for you. It smells like a slaughterhouse in there."

The uniformed men secured the front and back entrances, and were on their radios when back-up vehicles began to arrive on the scene. Within twenty minutes Tim and LB pulled up in a black sedan with a flashing red light.

"We're from homicide," Tim proclaimed, "what have you got for us so far?"

"Three bodies butchered and mangled and more red stuff on the floor and walls than I've seen in a long time. We've secured the place. No sign of anybody else inside, blood's congealed, must' a happened yesterday. These two visiting nurses just found the bodies and called in. It's almost unbelievable."

By the time the Chief arrived, forensics had started their work. LB and Tim had already taken statements from the home health nurses, who were recovering in their van. The Chief examined the scene and the bodies, working around the forensic team.

109

"One of these died of a broken neck," Tim surmised. "The second has a stab wound to the chest. Probably right in the heart, judging by the blood. He couldn't have lasted over a minute. The man in the bed over there is Charles O'Reilly. He lives...well, lived here. The visiting nurses came over because he had surgery last week and this would have been his initial home health visit."

LB continued, "The man in the bed was probably smothered with that pillow. It doesn't look like he was able to put up much of a fight. He also has a large wound out over the side of his left hip. There's not much blood there and you can see right down inside. 1 think the ball part of the hip bone is missing."

"Looks like the killer was carving up the man in the bed," Tim said, "when the other ones came in and interrupted him. I'm thinking we're probably looking at more than one assailant to do all this. He must have had some help."

The Chief returned to the nurses outside in the van.

"I can imagine the shock when you opened the door," he said. "I know you've seen a lot of trauma, but this is one of the worst for any of us. 1 just have a few questions I need to ask and then you can take off."

They uttered something that sounded like "Anything we can do to help," and he continued.

"Now, let me understand, why were you two here this morning?"

"We had orders to come out for a first time home health visit," Judy said. "Dr. Thomas replaced his hip last week. His chart said he'd had both hips replaced. That left one should have a metal orthopaedic device in there."

"We're going to need to talk to his doctor and try to get a little background and history on our victim. You know his first name?"

"Yes, it's John, but most people call him JC. We heard he was one of those exposed to the anthrax at the game Saturday, might still be isolated."

"LB, you want to get his address and phone number and I'll give him a call?"

"Sure, we'll track him down right away."

She had already flipped her cell and was dialing by the time he finished talking.

"Once you find him, I'd like to go out and talk to him as soon as possible."

The Chief asked the familiar question, "What do we know about the time of death?"

Tim was ready, "Forensics can help pin it down better later on, but from the condition of temps of the bodies, I'm thinking about 10:00 last night."

The Chief just nodded. Tim was learning.

******************

Out on Ridgeway, JC was looking and waiting as he saw his car screech to a stop near the curb in front of his house. Through the window, he watched Lauren get out of the car, clad in a plaid skirt and short jacket, and walk toward the house. He observed her hips tilting and rotating and pivoting with each graceful step—just the things any well-trained orthopaedic surgeon would notice—when he heard his front entry bell ring. A melodic "Pizza Girl" rang out before he could get the door open.

Her smile dazzled. He took the box and almost lifted her off the floor with his embrace. They fit together perfectly. Her cheek was soft and her hair smelled of sweet orange. She looked up at him with those blue eyes and he couldn't help but cover her lips with his. As the kiss deepened, she began to tremble. JC was lost in her. His phone rang but they didn't break apart until the message began to register and bring them back to earth.

"Dr. Thomas, this is Investigator Murray Lane, D.C. homicide. I need to talk to you. It's rather urgent, I'm afraid. If—"

JC snatched up the phone. "Hello, this is Dr. Thomas."

She could hear only his side and that was troubling enough.

"Oh no! He was such a nice man, only fifty-four years old. Sure, anything I can do to help."

He hung up and turned to face Lauren. "Seems like one of my postoperative patients was murdered last night, along with two other men," he said. "They're coming out to see if I could be of any help with his recent history."

"My God, John. I'm sorry. What else can happen?" She

111

looked at him sincerely and paused, "You know, you might be kind of bad luck…at least you provide me job security." She remarked, trying to lighten the solemn mood.

"I don't know why this is all happening or when it's going to end, but when this is all over, I want to pick up exactly where we left off."

When the three homicide investigators arrived, Lauren took the lead with introductions. She and Chief Lane knew each other well, and if the Chief was surprised at her presence, it didn't show. He was a very good detective.

"John, this is Chief Investigator Murray Lane. He worked with my dad some time ago. Chief, this is Dr. John Thomas, JC. We've been seeing each other lately and we were both exposed in the attack at the stadium. We've been taking our antibiotics and there's no evidence that we're contagious, but I thought you should know."

"I'm glad to see you're both well," the Chief said as Tim moved back a step.

"What's this about another homicide?" she asked.

The Chief briefly describe the horrible scene and the fact that Dr. Thomas had recently operated on Charlie.

"Yes, I just revised his hip last week. Nice man. I wouldn't think he'd have many enemies."

"Must have been a recall on the product, doc," Tim said. "He had a gaping wound over his left hip and it looked like something had actually been removed."

"Did you say left hip?"

"Yes."

"I did the right side. That left one was done several months ago overseas, and that side looked okay when I saw him in the hospital. Why would anybody want to kill him and steal a hip replacement?"

"We've got a serial killer working who's really weird," Tim rushed to explain. "Must'a seen it on the news. He's been removing body parts from the corpses left and right. It's been in all the papers, but we didn't tell them about the removals."

Lauren had been listening carefully.

"This is too much of a coincidence. John's office was

broken into last week and now one of his patients has been killed and a part of him taken. He saw the probable thief as he was leaving the scene of the robbery. We couldn't match it to any mug shots, but we've got a great sketch down at the office. That might not have been a break-in looking for drugs after all."

The Chief spoke slowly and thoughtfully, giving time to process, "We have reason to believe two of our Jane Does had recently been overseas. Could that be a connection?"

"Did they have surgery over there?"

"One had recent dental implants done somewhere," the Chief said. "Probably out of the country. The third girl was too mutilated to tell much."

"Any signs of an IV on her? Sometimes that'll scar the veins for a while."

"No needle tracks in the arms, pretty much rules that out," Tim reasoned.

"Maybe," LB wondered, "but when I had my knee scoped, they just put the IV in the back of my hand. That possible here?"

"Sure," J.C. inquired. "Pathologist say anything about that?"

"In addition to some other things, this guy amputated both hands on these two girls and took them with him so we couldn't get any prints," she replied.

"Well, if there were no scars, only other thing that might show up to indicate recent surgery would be some traces of anesthesia meds in the blood and tissue or some possible scratching in the windpipe where a tube was placed."

"We don't really want this getting out," the Chief added, "but after she was dead, the killer also severed her neck, and the whole head and throat are missing from the fifth vertebrae on up."

"That's terrible ... what a maniac," Lauren said. "What kind of person would do that?"

"The kind we've got to catch and catch soon," the Chief added.

"Dr. Thomas, you got any other thoughts?"

"Well, you know, most times that endotracheal tube they use during an operation will go well below that C-5 level of the neck. I'm sure the M.E. looked."

"LB— " was all the Chief said.

She was taking notes.

"You know," JC said. "I've got the prosthesis I took out of his right hip. I'd never seen one like it before. It was put in somewhere overseas. Outfit called Imperial Medical, information was on Charlie's PC. They took his laptop when they broke into our office, but I'd already copied his files. I didn't get very far when I talked to the hospital over there, but maybe you can. Contact info's on the disc.

"I'll get it and the prosthesis I took out for you. They're both out in the trunk of my car. I was going to take the implant to the office or out to the University to have some of the professors look at it more closely, but I got distracted. They've been in police custody."

"John!" Lauren exclaimed. "Good thing I didn't get pulled over for speeding. I might have had trouble explaining that thing. Anything else in there I should know about?"

As JC went to retrieve the items, the Chief of Homicide said, "Lauren, let's go down and have a look at that sketch, shall we? That man he saw wanted something from Dr. Thomas's office and now someone's been murdered to get this other hip.

"Tim, get ready to call your friends at the newspaper. I think we're going to need their help to publish this robbery suspect's picture. If we can find that man, we might also have our killer."

Chapter Twenty

Housed in a secure glass case on public display in the National Archives Building is a signed agreement that guarantees freedom of speech to all Americans. That promise is a small, but extremely important portion of a much more inclusive document that became the law of the land over two centuries years ago. The wide, famous avenue in front of the ornate building was subsequently named for this historic manuscript.

Looking out the back door of that building, one can see another heavily fortified structure, whose occupants could be put in prison for being too free with their speech. It was in this place that

Pat's group exercised another freedom as they peacefully assembled in a secure room. The time was precisely 16:00 on Monday.

In order to defend and secure this most open of all large countries on earth, certain secrets were to be carried by only certain segments of the population. The varying levels of this secrecy outnumbered the many layers found in a cake at an Inaugural Ball, although the icing was much more tempting. One of the hardest parts of Pat's job was ensuring that the invited guests got their full share of the cake from the proper layer without letting the crumbs and bits of frosting fall to the floor where they might be devoured or swept up and carried away by the insects bent on destroying the whole affair.

The 9/11 Commission Report recommended better communication between intelligence agencies, but rules of evidence and shared thoughts among individuals had previously exposed and neutralized valuable assets of these agencies. The icing on the cake was getting stickier and starting to run from the heat.

For these and other reasons, it was necessary to have only redacted versions of the group's report leave the conference room. The report made for very dry, but necessary reading as follows:

After careful questioning, the arena janitor voluntarily gave a great deal of useful information. His living quarters were also discovered, searched and the contents studied. It was ascertained that he had a very good counterfeit passport portraying his likeness and bearing the name Ali Franklin Norton.

The suspect recalls the name Ali from his childhood, but his family disintegrated shortly after he learned to walk and he never knew the rest of his original name, nor his place of birth. He was educated in a Madrasas and has been called by many different names, dependent on the circumstances.

The man has spent time in the Afghanistan-Pakistan border region in several terrorist training camps that no longer exist. He then traveled to the continent of Africa, and thence to England as a devout follower and a recruiter for his radical movement. Three years ago, he journeyed through the Caribbean and subsequently on to the central regions of Mexico. [see note one]

Working his way up through the mountains and across the desert of that country, he crossed Rio Bravo del Norte near its Great Bend. Ali thus entered this country illegally along with a number of other persons while certain authorities blinked. Once safely across the Rio Grande, he was picked up by a man he knew only as Kafeel and provided with the new passport proclaiming that he was an American citizen. [see note two]

The detainee and one other person, whose name Ali does not know, were driven by Kafeel to Washington, D.C., in a truck. Along the way, they made many side trips. Some of which he remembered. They had passed by the military facilities in San Antonio and close to a weapons plant at a swirling red river before leaving the state of Texas. They continued on across the next state and detoured to see a nuclear reactor making electricity. The journey took them near an air base where the powerful but invisible bombers rested before crossing a huge muddy river near the city with a giant arch.

Kafeel and the other one would occasionally leave Ali for a time while they visited certain other landmarks in the country. Many pictures were made and many notes were taken, but he had never seen the photographs nor read the notes. [See note three]

Once in the capital of the country, he was placed as a custodian for the stadium commission that managed the arena. He used the name Al. The man assumed some money was offered to have him hired in that position with no experience, but that was not his concern.

For two years, Ali was careful to warrant no police record. His bosses considered him to be a good employee who kept to himself; he worked hard and made no friends nor enemies. Recently, he was promoted to supervisor of a small crew whose task was to clean up and supply the restrooms and locker areas in the large building.

Some eight months before, during a vacation from work, he was summoned to Las Vegas to meet with Sheik xxxxxx, who was believed to be a high ranking radical cleric from xxxxxx. Current whereabouts unknown. [See note four]

At that time in the middle of the dry Mohave Desert, a cell that

116

had been slumbering inside the United States for at least three years, "yawned, stretched and rubbed their eyes when called to awaken. The many sins and excesses of the infidels were demonstrated" and Ali was there, instructed in the details necessary to perform his portion of the attack.

The prisoner recalls staying at a small hotel outside the brightly lighted city where prayer and the reading of the Book was continuous. He was startled one day when a group of powerful jet airplanes shook the earth as they flew overhead in extremely close formation, only a few hundred meters above the ground. The group knew they could not win against this military by direct warfare without a powerful ally, but terror attacks could erode any civilization.

Ali also remembers that he, Kafeel and one other person—again he does not know the name—were taken up in a helicopter on this trip. They were shown a very large dam that held a lake with enough water to satisfy millions of the infidels and to make power for the lights. Their flight then continued down between the walls of a huge deep rocky canyon that had been carved for centuries by a muddy river at the bottom.

The three were returned to the city for more reading and prayer. After another day, he was taken to the large airport where many people crowded through the security screening. There was no difficulty with the passport. He and Kafeel then returned to Washington in separate airplanes to wait patiently, with great anticipation. The cab driver delivered the supplies to him on the previous Sunday and he had no difficulty placing and activating the weapons as he had been trained.

The attendant was at the lowest levels of this cell. His only contact in the district was Kafeel, the driver, and he had no way to initiate their meeting. His job was to take the valuable materials that were brought to him, and process and install them in the soap dispensers and the hand dryers of certain restrooms. [See note number five]

Ali was to stand watch through the first and second basketball games and then leave the devices in place for a concert scheduled for the following night. He was to leave the city late Sunday night and then disappear before the anthrax could be discovered and

117

traced to him. By that time, many more would have been unknowingly contaminated and many more of the infidels would have died. He did not make it out of the stadium, though; he was exposed, shot in the back and captured.

The prisoner believes that several other individuals were designated as messengers or couriers and they would be his only contacts. The man he knew as Kafeel was the only person he had seen in Washington. He drove a taxi cab to their meetings which always took place outside secure areas at different sites. Ali had no knowledge of this man's hereabouts and last saw him on Sunday prior to the attack at the stadium.

He also thinks that there were two or more persons in the cell who were trained as assassins. He has never seen these persons, does not know their names and has no firm knowledge of where they might be located. He suspects that one might be in the Washington area and that one might be working in Canada. [see note number six]

The meeting eight months ago at a small hotel just outside Las Vegas was a religious revival for Ali. The cleric reinforced his religious beliefs and illuminated the greed and vanity found in the United States. The sheik brought an elaborate plan from the highest levels abroad to use the weakness of the Americans themselves to cause their destruction. The custodian thinks there might be two parts to this plan, but that was never confirmed to him. *He was assured that Jihad had been declared and that he was Mujahedeen, a holy warrior. Should he perish in this war, his place in Paradise was guaranteed with seventy virgins, all as pretty as his nurse, who were waiting to satisfy his every need.*

The man is still being held in isolation at a secret location with the designation of an enemy combatant. Doubtful that he has any more useful information.

> Status of most recent bioterrorism attack:
> Bacillus anthraces - strain to be determined
> 28,361 persons in attendance at the two events
> 532 yet to be located
> 1,174 confirmed of high-risk exposure
> 597 displaying symptoms, including spores

75 in critical condition from the first exposure
19 deceased
Attachments and notes:
Note number one: Detail to CIA, Interpol and British SIS MI 5 and 6 Box 850

Note number two: Release information to Dept of State INS.

Note number three: Alert local FBI field offices, ATF in said areas and Mil Intel

Note number four: Release to CIA and FBI SAC Las Vegas.

Note number five: Silicone encapsulated saline-gel containing materials housing the  spore form of anthrax - strain undetermined - modified from implants used for augmentation mammoplasty - sources unknown. 350, 450 and 550 cc volume, average 50,000 spores per cc Installed in soap dispensers and blow dryers for hands Modified to dispense a significant aerosolized dose of anthrax to the user. Alert FDA, ATF, Army Bio-weapons Ft. Dietrich.

Note number six: Release to Royal Canadian Mounted Police - security level three and above only.

Assessment of validity of report judged to be 91%.


After the report was read by all, one of the women spoke.
"Patrick, I don't want to know how you got this much from this man this quick, but your people deserve a medal."
"Well, it is what it is." Pat stated, "Now, it's obvious his handlers know we have him. There are pictures all over the news, and they'll have to assume that we'll turn him at some point. So we have to move very quickly. I've already got people looking for this taxi driver Kafeel.
"Daniel, can your personnel start working on the hi-res photo info from the camp areas he might have attended? Handle

with delicacy."

"Understood. If it gets out what camps we saw and what we're still seeing, we'll lose this advantage." he replied.

"I don't know how, I'm sure it's our capitalist system at work, but some of the press are very good at uncovering 'secret' data. They might already know that he got Afghan camper of the year," the grandmother said.

"Damn sure he wasn't voted most congenial, but I hope he was at least the runner-up for most photographic," the Colonel added.

"Bob," Pat said, "If you could follow the biology of this organism with the army and Public Health, the lab here and ATF will continue to look for an implant source. Now if there're no necessary questions, why don't you brief your need-to-know personnel and green light them to start digging? Let's plan to be back here at 06:00 unless we strike gold before then."

Chapter Twenty-one

Basil sat with a troubled mind on the floor of his darkened room while another snowstorm howled outside again. He had not slept. He knew that the authorities in the United States had tremendous resources and manpower. He had seen them in action. In spite of the time and money being spent on the investigation and recovery from the anthrax attack, his work of last night would draw significant new attention from the local police once the corpses were discovered. He was not seen and left no physical trail, so it could be several days before the reason for the dead men were found. He would know when that happened from the news reports.

It was unfortunate that he had been interrupted at his most recent victim's house. It would have served no purpose to make the remains of the three men disappear in the fire he had planned for O'Reilly. That would cover nothing and would have alerted the investigators straight away. These would be the first male bodies of his to be found in the area, and the connection to the spore-bearing women would still not be seen for a time. The police would be confused but would continue their plodding investigation. They would eventually become aware that the man named Charles had made several trips abroad for surgery. The people who examined Basil's victim would discover that the hip replacement had been removed. At some point, they would know that the last two women he left on the streets had been to a common hospital across the ocean and the link among the mutilated animals would be known.

The planners had done well to suggest that the first woman he butcher be far out of the district. The first in this area was completely at random and of no value but to waste the authorities' time and confuse their efforts. They would be searching for a disturbed sexual killer, not a devout soldier of jihad. She had been unknown to Basil, a fortunate opportunity arriving alone in Washington, selected only because of her pale skin. She had not likely traveled to a warm climate with sunshine recently, and if by chance she had been abroad, it would certainly not have been to the same country and area as the others. The confusion for the police would then be even greater.

There was no linkage to him or his group with her. The link was there with the next two women. The local police would never find it, but examination of the remains of this O'Reilly could bring significant new questions to light. Questions he did not want asked, yet.

There was another troubling fact. The metro police were at Dr. Thomas's house when he passed by the night before. Could they be coming closer? Not likely, but what were they doing there? There had been no way for them to make a connection to him, but he did not want another corpse to be discovered in the area at this time. The hunter must now plan carefully and execute quickly like a Cobra. The next body would be cold before the fang marks were seen. The trophy that the doctor had taken could wait for now. The thought of letting the doctor live caused Basil to seethe but he saw no other safe course to him. It was clear to the man where his next killing trip should be.

There was a target in the state to the south who had previously made more than one tour abroad. Her body contained two things that he desired. It would be an overnight journey, but Basil thought it best to be out of the metro area. He thought leaving any more signs in this district seemed foolish until the authorities' awareness faded.

His trophy case was empty; he needed to replenish it. The prizes got passed off as he collected them. This habit would continue, for they were much too valuable to be discovered. He knew Kafeel could be trusted so he changed the numbers on the door. Kafeel would make the arrangements needed for the next hunt.

This time, however, he turned two of the digits. He did not have time to wait for the taxi driver to pass. He did not want any risk that they would be seen together in this area. By moving more than one number, Kafeel would know they should not come together, yet. A cryptic note under the mat would give specific instructions for the time and place of their next meeting.

As usual, the killer did not require any weapons but his hands. The security checkpoints would be no barrier, even with cameras. He was still able to travel freely in this country and would use some of the money he had been given for his passage and any expenses. There would be no electronic footprints to be picked up and followed by even the most clever trackers. *Why should he leave any trail?* He did not need much and money came freely from Kafeel, the courier, and he used it wisely.

Basil stretched out on his rug at prayer time. He then dressed himself and inserted his brown lenses. He placed the protective coverings in the freshly cleaned backpack and then set out on foot for the train. He would slaughter the animal, harvest her parts and pass them on to the courier. The only difference this time was that he did not plan to use the victim's car for transportation. The courier would bring a vehicle in which to load and dispose of the body. This arrangement had been made by note.

His journey would take all night, but Basil was confident of his plan. He was a deadly and invisible holy warrior. The hunter would return the next evening successful and under the welcome cover of darkness. He would then resume his quest for the targets that remained near the district, especially the doctor.

Basil continued thinking. *Ali the janitor had been taken from the stadium by the Americans. He was weak and had been captured by a lowly woman no less. It was known that the man was not a true warrior and the plan all along had been to take him after he left the arena on Saturday night. Before the anthrax could have been suspected, his soul was to be sent on to Paradise. Now, he had been taken alive and could identify Kafeel, and he would tell his captors very soon. Ali could not be trusted. There were but a few hours for the cab driver to disappear.*

Several hours later, after the snow stopped, Kafeel came down the patched street lined with faded cars in front of Basil's flat. He observed the tilting of the numbers of the address and retrieved the waiting message as planned at their previous meeting. He had been quite busy during the last twenty-four hours.

As soon as the pictures of Ali's capture at the arena had been seen, Kafeel returned to his dwelling and purged the place of his tracks and his scent. The home address known to the cab company was a vacant warehouse. They had never checked, but the FBI would know very soon. They would know he drove a taxi. They could work very rapidly when necessary.

Moving with haste after cleaning his nest, Kafeel drove the cab southward down the Parkway named for the first ruler of this hated country who was a notorious Freemason. With the help of one other trusted person, they launched the taxi cab into the Potomac river. From there, the current would sweep it toward the bay with the other discarded items. Perhaps it would sweeten the oysters, but it possessed no useful evidence of his presence to offer.

Allah provided another means of transportation in the form of an old green pick-up truck with a camper shell attached. It was in that vehicle that Kafeel now traveled. He would stow the valuable weapons that the killers had obtained in a safe place known only to him, and continue to his next meeting place where Basil would be waiting with more trophies.

He felt secure as he drove south. Kafeel, the cab driver, became Mr. Smith, and the truck was registered in that name. It would be at least a fortnight before the previous owners would turn up missing and their bodies would never be found. He had a valid driver's license and even a passport, if needed, with his clean shaven likeness. These were expert documents; he had watched them being made. They were given to him free of charge by a close

friend who had recently retired from the tourism and travel
business.

*****************

Amid these whirling events, JC was at home in a much
more comfortable situation. Lauren had called to talk when she got
in from work. *It was kind of nice to have someone make rounds on
him for a change.*

"I just got off the phone with my sister in law and her kids,"
she said. "I've been staying away from them even though the
chance of me being infectious is real low. Wouldn't want to take
any risks with the small children."

"I know you miss them ... how many do they have?"

"Three. A six-year-old boy and a girl that just turned four.
The baby is a year old, and I think the older two are hoping he's a
rental and will need to be returned pretty soon, but they'll get over
it. With my brother gone a lot flying overseas, Ann really has her
hands full."

"Yeah, I can imagine." JC said. "Is your brother back home
yet?"

"No, since they shut down both the airports here, it's really
wreaking havoc with the schedules," she said. "He's staying close
and hoping to get out of Heathrow tomorrow."

"Maybe he'll get invited over to Windsor Castle?"

"He'd like to. He says the flag is up, so the queen's there
now. He figures she has cable and gets ESPN One, Two and even
Deportes."

"I can see her sitting there, with her face painted. I'm told
that she started the wave anyway. Big fan. With all the famous
millinery, I bet she has a cheese head or a hog hat in the closet
somewhere behind all those crowns."

Lauren laughed, and it reminded him of springtime at the
Vivaldi's before she continued, "Anyway, they keep trying to fix
me up; they think I should be married and raising children."

"Yeah, I'd be more interested in what you think."

"Well," she was open. "A few years ago I moved in with a
lawyer from the Prosecutor's Office. He left there, went into

124

private practice and wanted me to quit work and live my life around him. I was pretty close until I found out one of the other attorneys in their office, a woman named Sue Ann, and he were spending more time in the bedroom than in the courtroom. It's been a while, but I still can't laugh when I hear the one about the lawyer who got 'Sued'. There've been a few others before but that's it, in a nutshell. What about you?"

"Sounds a lot like yours except the names are changed to protect the few innocent. The most recent was a nurse. We were essentially married for a few years, except for the paper work. Then she quit her job one day. I'd come home dead tired or be on call and she'd want to go out and socialize--plays, symphonies, black tie charity things. I tried for a while until I realized she'd just as soon go out alone, but not necessarily stay out alone. Been a few short affairs, but mainly dinner with somebody's sister since then."

"Sounds pretty much the same," she mused, "and I really can't wait until we can get together again and take up where we left off."

"Maybe tomorrow? I'm a professional and really need to conduct a more thorough exam", JC quipped.

"I'd love to, but tomorrow really is going to be hectic around here." She sighed, "Homicide said they might need some extra help tomorrow on the phones. I'm guessing they caught a break in the serial case, but don't quote me on that. They sure have been pacing around a lot more today than usual."

JC persisted, "Well I really do want to see you, again, soon."

"Tell ya what…if you don't mind waking up early Wednesday morning. Like 5 a.m. then I'll swing by and bring you some coffee before I have to head into work."

"Are you kidding?" JC perked up, "I usually have to get up at that time for bad news. Heck, for you and coffee. No problem."

Chapter Twenty-two

JC woke early Tuesday morning. It was too early according to his steadfast and reliable digital friend slumbering on the nightstand. He was grateful that neither he nor Lauren had any noticeable evidence of disease. They resumed their immunizations and were taking their ciprofloxacin without fail. He had no schedule, no need to be at one or more places at the same time, but he was eager to get up and see what he could learn today. JC was following the recommendation that he stay away from patients and the general public for at least another week. *Thank God for his partners.* After all, many of the people he dealt with in his profession were already in a weakened condition, sick or elderly. Even though the chance of his transmitting the deadly bacteria was extremely small, the risk could not be ignored.

JC didn't really have a need for espresso. He knew he could stop drinking coffee at any time, but it did smell so good in the mornings. Plus, the surgeon general couldn't decide: it might actually be good for you. With that in mind, he put in enough water for at least two large cups.

Since the paper hadn't come yet, he decided to do a little research on anthrax. He went out the little-used side door, past the hot water heater compartment, into the attached double garage and tried to remember where to look. The search took him through three dusty cardboard boxes, past the underlined books of gross anatomy and organic chemistry, before he found the old notes on microbiology from both college and med school. His reward for not having cleaned the garage this winter was doubled when he also found some forgotten receipts for charitable contributions. He'd need those in another few weeks, so he carefully marked that box before going back into the house.

He finished the first cup and reviewed the material he had retrieved. By that time, the local paper had arrived. He carefully prepared a second coffee and then sat back to read the news. He had time today for the whole thing.

On the front page of the paper was a familiar face staring back at him. There were two pictures. One was a facial drawing, and while you could never do justice to those yellow eyes in print, the artist had done a skillful job of rendering recognizable features. There was a second sketch of what JC had remembered of the man's attire, complete with backpack. JC pouted, *this must be the reason why I won't see Lauren until tomorrow morning. I can't say that it isn't urgent.*

The words under the pictures informed the public that this

man was wanted for questioning. A brutal homicide had taken place at a given Georgetown address around ten o'clock Sunday night. If anyone had any information regarding the man shown above or his whereabouts, would they please contact District of Columbia Homicide Division. All calls would be handled anonymously. JC thought *it's hard to believe that anything to do with Charlie could be anonymous, obviously the writer had never met his friend.*

There was a second significant article on the front page that presented some follow-up to the terrorist attack at the arena. Of the estimated 35,000 people who had attended one of the two ball games, some two thousand were believed to have been exposed. Over a thousand people were still unaccounted for and over a hundred were dead, but that number could not be confirmed. If anyone else had reason to suspect that they had been exposed, they should contact the FBI or their local doctor immediately. JC wondered what the actual numbers were, but the paper usually came within two or three times of the truth, and obviously a lot of families had been affected.

Of the 90 or so strains of anthrax that JC knew to exist from his reading, this one had yet to be positively identified. It had significant characteristics of the Ames strain, which was thought to have killed six people of the postal service just a few years before. An American committed that attack for reasons that were not yet clear.

Ames, named after the city in Iowa, was apparently the pit bull of anthrax and might prove to be even more virulent than the Vollum strain that had been isolated for biologic warfare in the United Kingdom a number of years ago. Vollum was known to be available in many unfriendly labs around the world. It wasn't hard to grow if you wanted to take the risks. The article went on to note that symptoms might develop four days after exposure. In other cases it could take up to two months before symptoms would occur.

JC knew that anthrax was a very durable beast. When its environment was threatened, it could form spores with thick walls, which could remain dormant for decades. Once these spores came in contact with a host, in this case through the respiratory tract or a cut in the skin, they could multiply rapidly. Without treatment, they would produce poisons which could kill eighty-five times out of a hundred.

The article went on to say that if the authorities knew the origin of this weapon or how it got in the stadium they were not giving out that information. Be assured, no expense was being spared in the investigation or the treatment of those exposed.

Fortunately, the press simply referred to JC as "an alert fan" who happened to be at the basketball game. Unfortunately, they referred to Lauren as "Lt. Lauren Long, a true heroine of the police department" Thankfully, the newspaper had not identified him but he knew Lauren hated the attention.

JC had lots of time on his hands as he sipped his coffee, and relapsed into an old habit of reading the editorial page. There he learned, "that several secret memos were known to exist. Had the FBI released them, it was likely that this tragedy would have been completely averted.

"Surely the Commander-in-Chief was briefed last year and should not have been wasting the tax payers hard-earned dollars traveling in the South and Midwest at the time of the attack. A bipartisan congressional committee should be appointed to look into this debacle."

A second opinion agreed in principle, but blamed this all on the CIA and the two previous administrations.

JC rapidly turned to "Sports" to read about ice hockey and boxing, contests that had some rules and demonstrated much less hostility than editorial opinion writing. There he found the wrap-up on basketball.

With the clock running out last Saturday night in the overtime period and the home team trailing by a point, the guard with the previously injured ankle put up a shot that missed badly—"probably due to lingering trouble with the ankle," the writer speculated. The eighth man off the bench, who averaged 1.7 ppg, dutifully blocked out under the basket, rebounded the ball and had a put back at the buzzer to win. "The monumental climb from the cellar to first place and a play-off birth would certainly earn the coach a contract extension." The writer surmised. The team, however, had to forfeit the first three games of their post-season due to the quarantine; effectively ending their season because the first series would have been the best out of five. JC thought, *that will probably cost someone a seat come November.* He reached for the tissue box to wipe his nose. He had just started sneezing.

******************

Five hours away that morning in a rural community in North Carolina, Melva was coming out from under the dryer at the Puff and Fluff Beauty Parlor.

"So, Mel, big date coming up?" the proprietor of the shop asked as she was taking out the large rollers.

"Not 'til Friday," Melva said with a hint of pride. "I been asked out to the dance at the lodge."

"You think you're up to that with the surgery on your hips?"

"Yeah, it's been well over five weeks since the last operation. I need to go out with a man and make sure these things work. A test drive, so to speak."

All five ladies in the room cackled. There were no secrets at a beauty shop where the First Amendment rights ran rampant.

"Going overseas to have my hips replaced was the best thing I could have done, since I was left with no insurance. Met a lot of people in the same situation. One of the nicer men from Washington is going to come down to see me when he gets better. I expect he'll be calling in the next week or so."

"Well, you go on out and have a good time," the proprietor said. "You deserve it. What's it been? 'Bout two years since that sob left?"

"Nearly two and a half," Melva said. "Right after I turned fifty."

"Say, if you want me to comb you out Friday, just come on in. No charge."

"Thanks, I might. I better run on to the store now. I'm completely out of milk and dog food."

After two stops, Melva pulled under the carport next to her white frame house and started in with her twenty-five pound sack for the dog. She decided it would be better to make one trip with

129

the heavy sack and then come back for the rest of the items, since her first hip was aching more today, and she was limping a bit on that side.

That hip was done over three months ago, but had been bothering her more this last week. *Probably from carrying the dog's food*, she thought. *I should sell him.* Melva was tough and determined but she would never separate from that dog if she could help it. Her Friday date for the dance would not be canceled. It'd feel better by then. She'd just take some of that headache powder she kept for emergencies and push on.

As she approached the front door, she called to her best friend. He was a yellow lab who guarded the house when he wasn't asleep under the chair inside the house. Usually he came with his whole body wagging to meet her, especially if she had food, but not this time.

She opened the door and called, "Huck ... Huck ... you better not be on my bed."

Melva made it to the kitchen before she saw her pet bleeding from the neck and lying motionless on the rug. Her jaw flew open to call out for help, but Melva's mouth did not have time to close. The skull under the newly done hair shattered from the powerful blow, and she joined her beloved companion on the floor.

Basil was unmoved. His only concern was to proceed with care to ensure he didn't nick or scratch the implants. The two hips did not require him to use any special technique. He just opened the skin through the scars and pulled the flesh apart--the quicker the better. The metal stems pulled out easily from the bone on both sides. No special clean up required. There was no good way to cover this one up, but he would be out of the state, never to return before the carcasses were found.

The killer considered mutilating the woman's chest, but didn't want any similarities to the women in Washington. Instead he made two very deep slashes in her belly in the shape of a cross. That should give the police something to think about for a while. Basil went outside. There was no one for miles around. He removed his gloves and coverings before he carried the valuable parts of the woman over the hill in his pack.

After he reached the small back road shown on his map, it

took him a minute or two to identify his ride sitting at the appointed place. Kafeel was now clean-shaven and driving a familiar looking green pickup truck with a camper shell over the back bed.

The two men traveled together unnoticed for a hundred miles. They had been far removed from the capital for over twenty-four hours and felt safe in this rural area. They talked about the old times they had spent together half-way around the world and shared with some glee the results of the anthrax. They agreed that Ali could have done much better and since his capture, plans had to be changed somewhat, but the result from the next event would be devastating to the Americans.

Kafeel dropped Basil off to walk back to a train station he had never used for his return trip to Washington. He still had work to do there with the harvest, besides they would meet again soon. The time of the next attack was drawing near. Most of the weapons had been received. The infidels would be surprised when the next blow was struck. It would be the most deadly by far and would bring this government to its knees.

Kafeel, now Mr. Smith, would stop by his storage facility near the district to move the necessary supplies out of the area for a while. The FBI could not trace the collected items and would not know about the plan until it was much too late. The pickup truck with the camper covering the bed would provide the ideal means of transportation.

Chapter Twenty-three

It had stopped snowing during the night, and the canopy of darkness was changing to a gray overcast sky. The dawn temperature was above freezing for the first time in weeks, and the assortment of people who lived and worked in the metro area were returning to their Tuesday morning chores by train, bus or bumper-to-bumper. For most, it was a normal busy work day, a chance to resume the familiar routine of any large city. Up-and-comers were busy gathering data and preparing reports, while their executives were holding meetings over freshly squeezed juice and bottled water. Attorneys were citing cases and dragging out arguments in their briefs, which were anything but. Buyers and sellers of goods were engaged in the contact sport of capitalism, while those in the service industry—nurses, doctors, religious leaders, trash collectors and cops among others—were servicing the people.

LB had come in to the office promptly at seven followed by the Chief and then Tim, with his coffee, at about eight. The tip hotline at district headquarters had been ringing continuously for two hours by that time. The morning newspaper had hit the streets about five o'clock with the artist's drawings and a brief account of the triple homicide at the O'Reilly place on the front page. That had launched an avalanche of new calls to the police.

More people were needed at the headquarters building just to keep up, but the department was stretched and under-staffed already. It was even worse in the wake of the anthrax attack. Screening the messages was a time-dissolving and difficult task. Each call had to be carefully evaluated. It was hard to know which one might produce that nugget that could break the case wide open.

There were the usual calls from the curious. There were calls with a lot of "mights" and "maybes" and "I thinks." These were people wanting to be helpful, but who were probably mistaken in their information. These tips were especially hard to evaluate, because often the seemingly insignificant little observances of the people, when pieced together, were the keys to locating a suspect.

There were calls from the wannabe detectives looking for their fifteen minutes and several free-lancers with more questions than answers, who could turn a few first-hand facts into a best seller. Some anonymous callers took the opportunity to suggest that it was their worst enemy, and he should be locked up right away. Several of the callers inquired about the amount of the reward, as if they might identify a brutal killer, but only if it would be worth their time and trouble.

In the midst of all of these, there were two very promising calls that required immediate follow-up attention. The Chief and his assistants listened to those recordings several times in the conference room. They needed to interview these people in person and show them the original drawings of the suspect. Being able to see the interviewees in person greatly helped improve the assessment of the information they provided.

Early on, there had been a call from a man named Muhammad who spoke with a bit of an accent and left a message. He was certain that he recognized the man pictured on the front page. The caller was still at work on his delivery job and would not be able to come in for several hours, but he would come to the district headquarters when he finished his schedule.

By 8:00 am, a second potential useful call had been received, this one from a taxi driver. He remembered picking up a man at about midnight on Sunday a little over a mile from the address listed and taking him all the way out to a convenience store near the beltway. "No, he didn't mind coming to interview at the headquarters," he proclaimed. Business was slow, and within an hour, he was at the station talking to the detectives.

The Chief had learned long ago that cab drivers could be very helpful, as some maintained strict logs of time and distance. They covered large areas of the city and were exposed to a great number of people. They kept reliable records and had good memories for faces and places. Many did not want to become involved with the police, thinking that what people did was their business as long as they paid the fare, but most understood the danger of having a spree killer on the loose. They didn't want one riding in their back seats, going from one murder to the next; as this patron had possibly done.

This particular cabbie had been driving in the city for a number of years and seemed very reliable. He took his time and carefully studied the artist's original sketches. While he'd never gotten a good look at the passenger's face, the build, dress and backpack were all familiar. He'd checked his records. He picked up a fare at 12:16 am on the night in question, nine blocks from the Georgetown address of the murder scene listed in the paper.

He remembered because it seemed like a long trip to nowhere. The passenger didn't talk at all the whole ride, and paid in cash with a good tip. He didn't take the receipt. The last he saw of the man was at a convenience store way out at the Ridgeway ramp, some 45 minutes away from where he was picked up, and it didn't look like his neighborhood nor did he act like it. In fact, the man almost seemed to be observing his surroundings for the first time. He seemed to study them.

Tim interrupted the narrative with, "Ridgeway! That's—" before the Chief rolled his eyes and broke in.

"Ridgeway, let's see, that's out by the beltway isn't it?"

If the taxi driver even noticed the exchange, he just let it ride.

"Yes. I didn't hang there very long. No chance to get another fare way out there at that time of night, so I don't know what he did after I dropped him off."

The cabbie had no other information about his whereabouts or who the man might be, but if he thought of anything else, he'd call back.

The Chief thanked the man for his cooperation. He'd been a great help, and they might need him again, if he could keep himself available.

As soon as the door closed, LB, with uncharacteristic emotion, started talking excitedly.

"Ridgeway, that's where Dr. Thomas lives, right out by the belt."

The street directory was already coming up on her computer screen. Tim returned to his favorite task of placing push pins on the wall map.

"Look!" he said. "The store where the cabbie dropped off his fare is just three blocks from Dr. Thomas's house. O'Reilly was his patient! That's way too much for a coincidence. "

"Not likely by chance, is it?" the Chief replied. "LB, why don't you get out to that store and see if they have any security tapes you could review? Maybe somebody out there can help us identify this guy. Oh, and let's check the cab companies for a pickup around that beltway store at about, say, 1:00 or 2:00 a.m."

The Chief continued, "A lot of this seems to center around Lauren's friend Dr. Thomas, doesn't it? After we talked with him yesterday, I looked at this hip replacement thing he gave us. I sure can't tell much about it, so I called one of my friends at the FBI lab out in Virginia. They're swamped of course, but he owes me a really big one and said he'd take a look, see if they can help us. Tim would you mind running it out there along with that backup disc we got from the doctor?"

"Glad to, Chief."

He'd never been inside, but now Tim was on his way to the famous FBI forensic lab with a blood-caffeine level well above the legal limit.

By mid-morning, one of the earlier phone-ins, the man who called himself Mo, came into the station. He was a friendly man, a native of Pakistan who was proud of the fact that he had legally immigrated to this country eight years before with his wife. He worked nights at a 24-hour grocery not too far from the projects and delivered newspapers throughout the city in the wee hours of the morning.

After seeing the artist's sketch on every stack of papers he'd distributed earlier that day, he was sure that he knew this man. He thought they might come from the same part of the world. Mo did not know his name, but he sometimes came into the store to buy food.

"He would not talk but to say, 'leave me alone.' I tried to bring him for prayer at the mosque half a year ago, but he would not be bothered. That is the man. I am sure, but he has brown eyes that change color on occasion."

Muhammad continued, "I have seen him walking on the streets with the backpack at different times, often very early in the morning or very late at night. There are not many people out then, the streets are deserted, but I use the back ways to stay on time with my papers. I see him coming and going from a brownstone apartment. The address is 2109, but you must look carefully. Sometimes the numbers twist in the wind."

As Mo got up to leave his frustration overtook him. He turned to the Chief, "You know something that people don't seem to consider about a man like this. He's obviously willing to use other people's lives to get what he wants but they don't consider that he's using people like me and my family as human shields. We might not directly be in danger of gunfire, but we are directly in danger of public disdain, which can sometimes lead to the other."

The Chief stood up, looked at the man and nodded his head. "Yes. Sadly you are absolutely correct. I don't know what consolation it is, but if this is the killer that we're looking for, know that I thank you as one American to the next," he said as he shook Mo's hand.

Although the man seemed sincere and accurate about his information, the Chief thought it was too early to saturate the neighborhood, even if they had the personnel, which they didn't. If this was their suspect, he was obviously extremely dangerous. They did not want to miss their chance by spooking him too early, giving him a chance to run. It would be better, for now, to send out a surveillance team to watch the house.

By the time the early darkness approached, the two-man stakeout was in place, concealed on a side street with a good view of the front door of the brownstone. The rooms seemed empty. There were no lights on, the shades were closed, and the street was nearly deserted in the cold weather. The two officers, in their dull, poorly painted car huddled down in their jackets with a thermos of black coffee, to do what they did best: blend.

The Chief, sworn to protect and serve, called JC at home. "Strict confidence, Doctor, plus we might still need some information from you," he explained as he repeated the story about the taxi driver's delivery of a passenger to the belt line near Ridgeway. While they did not know the significance, if there was any, he was advised to take extra caution. Did he have a gun? Security system? A dog? Of course, he should make sure all the doors and windows were locked before he went to sleep and call if he saw anything remotely suspicious. The Chief promised to promptly update him with any new developments in the case.

JC was not prone to panic, but he was prudent. He had seen that face up close. He unlocked the gun safe and selected the twelve gauge. He didn't think he would need it, but he loaded the shotgun and placed it near the bed anyway. Then he went back into the garage and re-locked the outside door and windows.

As an after-thought, he opened the door to the small compartment where the hot water heater was located. 'Hadn't looked in there for over a year, he thought, but it wouldn't hurt to check. Sometimes those things could leak.'

Still sneezing and congested, he really wanted to call Lauren, but he didn't need to worry her, and the Chief had said to tell no one. First thing she'd ask was, "How are you feeling?" and he wasn't a very good liar. Besides, she was a professional in that

136

area and she'd know right away.

*Let's see,* JC thought as he lay back in bed. *Recently his life threatened with a very large knife, exposed to anthrax and his office robbed. There was a killer who had murdered three people, including one of his patients, roaming the neighborhood, and the woman that he was beginning to love might also have the deadly disease. Back to the basics.* He followed the classic advice. Take a decongestant and two aspirin and wait for her to call upon him in the morning.

\*\*\*\*\*\*\*\*\*\*\*\*\*\*\*\*\*

Things went as planned for Basil. He made the long return trip with no difficulty to this point, but he'd been out of town over twenty-four hours. The target had been easily killed and he had used the scars over her hips for the harvest. The police would eventually find that parts of the skeleton were missing but would not know the significance of that for some time. Kafeel was there in the green pick-up truck, just as he had planned, without drawing suspicion. The courier took the pack with the two valuable items for storage. Basil knew this man could be trusted with safe hiding of the weapons until the time came for their use.

Basil had returned to Washington on the train, and then taken the bus for a ways. When he glimpsed toward the front of the bus, he saw something that startled him. Without drawing attention he peeked just long enough at a woman reading a newspaper to catch his own likeness on the front page. He knew the next 24 hours would be critical.

Sometime after midnight, he walked back into his neighborhood, satisfied with his work but furious about his unwanted attention. His eyes were more irritated than they had been for some time. His vision was blurred from the constant watering, and he did not see the men watching him as he turned the house numbers back vertical.

The killer quickly unlocked his door and checked for any sign of intruders. He needed to remove his contact lenses. Once that was done, he could prepare for his next hunt. Basil did not need much vision to sharpen his knives; that was done by feeling the blades. He moved the stone across the small, almost scalpel sized metal. This short instrument was best for removing breast implants, where too large or too deep cuts might rupture the underlying sack and allow the deadly anthrax to escape. He did not need this tool for his potential next target, though. Next, he worked to sharpen the steak knife to a fine edge. He used this instrument to harvest hip implants. It was perfect for slicing through flesh without much risk of damage to the metal prize inside--he would not need this one, either.

Lastly he placed in his backpack the large threatening butcher knife. Basil wanted the implant that the surgeon had removed from O'Reilly. It had not been at his office; he must search the man's home now that the police would be gone. Basil hoped to find the man alone in the house when he went to make his search. An encounter with this man would save him valuable time later. The sturdy, sharp blade was especially good for a close-in kill. It would cause the look of terror that he wanted to leave on the doctor's face.

After the sharpening work was done, Basil lay back on his hard bed to rest his reddened eyes for a few minutes before setting out. He only had about five hours before daylight. Due to his recent appearance on the papers around town he knew he should not wait for light to hunt again. He must get that piece and then finish out his part of the plan.

The hunter had not picked up the scent of his two stalkers as they waited outside in the car, nor had he heard the sounds of the camera as it captured his likeness when he had entered his cave. The killer could not know that he had become the prey, and he could not see his image flying through the cold night air to the Homicide Division of the District Police Headquarters.

Chapter Twenty-four

Years of doing certain actions and behaving certain ways breeds a sixth sense for people when doing those things. Basil had spent years hunting and being hunted. Although he did not know he was being monitored and his weariness from his recent trip out of state caused him to not check his tracks as he normally entered his brownstone apartment. His gut, nonetheless, told him to leave for his next journey out the passageway he had so cleverly created under the floor.

He pulled aside the ordinary looking rug in the middle of his floor. Underneath lay a steel reinforced trap door. So as to hide its appearance, Basil had built the hinges so that the door opened downward. A thick metal bar slid into a groove that he had carved out of the surrounding floorboard. So as to not even create a small divot and suspicion for anyone standing on the rug that covered the door, he placed a small metal piece that filled the slot that the metal bar left behind when it was locked.

Basil kept a metal rod that had a little hook at the end in the corner to help close the door when it was not in use. The bar could be slid from either inside or outside the door to allow for him to exit without leaving his apartment unsecure. Besides, no one knew of this passageway because it did not appear on any of the original building plans.

Once under the floor he crawled along a small tunnel underneath the apartment's first floor. After about twenty feet he came upon the exit he had built to the outside world. Another door upright with a similar design stood in front of him. This door was much heavier. The back of this vertical little door was covered with brownstone that matched the apartment. When he slid the door free he immediately ran into a metal wall.

He pushed the wall forward--it moved rather easily. Then when the metal impediment was far enough out of the way he stood up. He quickly looked around the pitch black back alley for occupants but he saw none. Feeling certain of his being alone, he pulled the door back into place and restored the metal dumpster that hid that part of the wall that had just granted him exit. Basil knew he must seldom use this passageway and never during daylight. Also, he only used it at night, if he knew it was a new moon and too cold for homeless people to be sleeping in the area.

Basil knew he had to get moving quickly. He had less than five hours to get to the doctor's house before sun-up. Fortunately, he did get to sleep a portion of the trip back from killing the last prey. Kafeel had done all the driving for that part of the journey. Making this current trip entirely on foot, however, would take most of the time remaining.

Avoiding all public transportation was a necessity until he acquired the trophy and got it to a safe place. He especially didn't want to use cabs because of their intimacy and lack of cover for camouflage from the driver. Also, he began to suspect that his last cab was the reason that he was now being hunted. After he accomplished this task, however, nothing else really mattered. He would disappear and head into another region far away in this vast, defiled country where he could continue the work set out for him by Allah.

No one knew of his departure from his brownstone cave as he crept out the back alley. Before leaving he had consulted his maps and committed them to memory. He knew better than to come out of the darkness or use any lights to consult directions to the doctor's home; either of these actions would draw him into the public eye. Although Basil knew the attention he now garnered in the city jeopardized the plan, he felt a great surge of adrenaline. He had before hunted in regions with deadly prey that knew his presence was near, and he had succeeded in those situations. He checked himself; *this is bigger than my own wants. This is for Allah and the other holy warriors, I must make this up to them because of my failure to keep to the shadows, if only I'd killed Ali sooner. Too late for that now, time to move ahead to bigger things.*

The time he had spent in this city, lying dormant, had been well spent. All of his maps not only included streets but also alleyways and paths that could only be travelled by foot. As he moved along his course with great stealth and agility he considered the details of how to proceed once he got to his destination. He did not lose focus while he considered the plan for his arrival. Before he came near any man-made structures, he would survey the terrain for signs of people. More importantly he would survey the terrain for fences that might contain dogs—the ultimate nighttime alarm system.

After nearly four hours he knew he was approaching the woods behind the doctor's neighborhood. Before entering the thicket he looked over at a house with an open garage and without a fence. He noted two cars in the driveway—neither looked useful for transporting a family. If it came down to it this would be his exit strategy. He then passed by that house and into the strip of trees that backed up to his destination.

Basil inched along the side of the house to get a view of the driveway. *Excellent*, he thought, *only one car and no police*. He noticed some of the lights on and as he snuck back around to the posterior he thought he heard movement within the house. Still covered in shadow he peeked through a bedroom window to see the doctor coming down the hall toward him. Basil noticed the clock on the stand reading, "4:45." The doctor entered the room, got some clothes from a dresser and went into the bathroom, shutting the door behind him. Basil heard the shower begin to run—with the doctor awake but in the shower Basil knew this the perfect time to enter the home, and any motion detector security system would be disabled. *Allah is good*, he thought as he quietly pried the bedroom door open that connected to the patio on which he was now standing. The lock made a tiny, "Click," as it turned sideways allowing admittance into the house. He entered, then locked the door behind him.

Constantly listening for the sound of the water to stop or the bathroom door to open Basil silently moved from room to room searching for both the trophy and any other person's presence. After a quick search of all the rooms he located neither. He found himself in the kitchen when he heard the water stop. Squatting behind the island in the middle of the room, he pulled out the butcher knife from his pack.

In the other room, JC opened the bathroom door. Wearing only his slacks, he grabbed his shirt from the hook on the bathroom wall. He thought, *Maybe I should toast some bagels?,* as he walked barefoot down the hall, fumbling to button his shirt.

Just after he rounded the corner to the kitchen he felt a crushing grasp knock him against the counter next to the refrigerator. The sounds of the coffee mugs crashing down from their hooks underneath the cabinets shattered the quiet of the early morning. Bewildered and terrified, JC quickly recalled his current status as being stalked. *Damn decongestant*, he thought as his assailant stepped forward with his knife to his throat.

"I know that you are a surgeon. You should know that I am also a surgeon," Basil looked into JC's eyes. He continued, "What you don't know is that you have something that I want. Something that Allah wants. Do you know what that is?"

JC, pinned against the counter with the blade at his throat, dared not move. He replied, "I have some idea."

Basil slashed JC across the cheek, just enough to cause a small incision. The blood took a moment to reach the surface of the skin and trickle down JC's face. Basil stated, "Now you *see* that I am a surgeon. And ideas aren't good enough."

With his face stinging from the laceration, JC knew he had no choices, no outs. He had to tell him exactly what he knew.

"If you are looking for the hip implant that I removed from Charlie O'Reilly or the disk that I copied from his files. I don't have them anymore."

Basil flinched at hearing that the man's laptop had files that had been copied. He didn't know what information could be on them, but didn't like the fact that this doctor thought it was what he himself was after. *I must tell the leaders about this revelation urgently,* he thought. His thoughts turned back to his prize.

"Where is the metal piece that you took out of the big man before I could claim it?"

Defiantly JC stated, "D.C. Metro Homicide Division."

Furious and overcome with rage, Basil pulled back the butcher knife to plunge it into JC's heart. Just as the knife cocked backwards, he saw the flash of the blade off the kitchen lights and heard a thunderous, "POP!" The sound of something shattering behind him and the spattering of blood on his face brought JC clarity, *that flash of light had not come from the knife.* He saw a familiar sight. Lauren stood in the kitchen entrance archway with her knees slightly bent and her gun still smoking.

The force of her shot through Basil's arm caused three things to happen--he dropped the knife behind him, his body got spun around toward the hallway leading to the bedroom and JC's coffeemaker shattered as the bullet continued on its trajectory into the kitchen wall. Without hesitation Basil continued down the hallway to make his escape from where he had entered.

With Basil out of her view, Lauren saw the blood rolling down JC's face. She made certain that the attacker didn't double back as she ran over to check the severity of JC's wounds. She knew that if he had serious injuries he would have to be tended to at once. She wanted to pursue the perpetrator but knew that with no one else around any serious blood loss could be fatal.

Quickly assessing the damage she pulled out her cellphone and contacted dispatch.

"This is Lt. Long at 4400 Ridgeway. I need medical and back-up units. We have a highly dangerous fugitive in the area. Also, find Chief Lane and have him contact me immediately."

"Lauren you have amazing timing. How did you get here when you did?" JC asked in a numbed state due to shock.

"I was out front when I heard a crashing noise a few minutes ago. When I went home last night Chief Lane told me that they had an eye on this guy at his apartment, but something about that sound disturbed me. I went to the front door and heard angry voices so I picked the lock and snuck in." She paused and asked sincerely, "Didn't you remember we had a date for me to bring you coffee this morning?"

"Well I did up until the point that another crazed man pulled another big knife on me with the intent of gutting me. I guess I was distracted," he said with some remorse for offending her.

She looked at him tenderly and spoke, "We'll let it go this time. I'm glad you are not really hurt."

With Lauren, in person this time, keeping guard over JC they waited for the EMT and back up. As Lieutenant, she wanted to begin the hunt while the trail was still fresh. As Lauren Long, she wanted to stay beside JC. Furthermore, she knew that "to protect" came first and so she stayed in place.

Tragically, the neighbors that lived in the house that Basil had already cased for his emergency get away fell out of her scope of knowledge. No one protected them. Basil merely saw them as a quick means to transportation. Then, to eliminate the scent of his trail for his pursuers, he killed them.

Chapter Twenty-five

Hunched over his desk on the third floor of the district headquarters, the Chief had returned to the office at four o'clock on Wednesday morning to study the results of the long range camera.

Leaning forward in the chair helped to eliminate the glare on his monitor from the overhead spotlights. After concentrating for a while in that position, it caused quite a strain to the back of his neck. He'd put in the next budget request for a new screen with adjustable tilt, but for now all he could do was get up on the desk and unscrew the offending bulb.

The Chief had completely recovered from his upper respiratory symptoms and decided that he might not even take the flu shot next year. It didn't seem worthwhile if he was going to get a cold anyway, but he'd wait to decide. He needed to talk it over with his wife. She was the one who kept up with the latest medical recommendations.

Although they'd been captured at some distance during the nighttime darkness, the images on his monitor, after being enlarged, brightened and enhanced, were considerably more detailed than the artist's sketch. The two person team had done a good job of filming; it certainly looked like the same individual whose picture was on the front page. He definitely looked suspicious, turning the numbers of his address and checking around his front door for signs of an intrusion before entering the apartment in the middle of the night.

The facial features were being run through the various digital image recognition systems, but that would take some time. There were so many security cameras in the region that there probably would be some hits, or at least a few electronic droppings along the trail. For now the suspect was in his den. Where he'd been last night before midnight was a matter of considerable concern to the homicide detective. There had been only one report to his division of a death the night before; it was by gunshot. The victim was a habitual drug addict with a constantly updated rap-sheet; tragically, his early death almost seemed inevitable. No other bodies had turned up, yet.

LB had interviewed the convenience store employees the day before, and they had no knowledge of the man the taxi driver dropped there shortly after midnight on Sunday. Their parking lot surveillance tapes showed no images of the individual, and the local cab companies had no record of a pickup near the Ridgeway address on the night in question.

Likewise, the Chief had not heard from the FBI forensic lab about the metal hip prosthesis that Tim delivered. At some levels, there was still a barrier between the feds and local law enforcement, but the Chief's old friend at the lab would let him know his findings when he could. Sometimes, he knew, there could be an amazing amount of information data-mined from a simple computer source, but it might take a while to retrieve everything from the disc holding Charlie's backed-up files.

The Chief was a product of the old school, back when the best detectives wore trench coats and roamed the streets. They relied on their gut feelings and played their hunches. While he was still aware of those feelings, things had changed considerably. He'd come to trust the results from the electronic data systems, even though he didn't fully understand all of the functions necessary to produce those results. That's what the computer savvy techs would provide, and they could cover so much more ground than his mentors could have, without getting a discarded wad of Topps on the bottoms of their Walkovers.

The Chief did, however, still understand the importance of hard work, persistence, and checking his facts. He also understood a lot about people. So, before he called the prosecutor and made an arrest that might not stick, he wanted to be very sure. It was time to call Muhammad, the one in the newspaper business, and Dr. Thomas to ask them to come in for verification.

Mo was just starting his morning route and was only a short distance from the station. He said he hated breaking his routine but understood the importance of his assistance. He came right in and studied the pictures carefully. This was the man he knew to frequent the brownstone. They had similar complexions and facial features, except the man on the screen had no beard.

Some time ago, the two men could have been born and lived in the same region of the world, but Mo had not seen that man nor his people in Washington before this year. If this man were proven to be the brutal killer then that fact would explain why he had refused to go with Mo to the mosque. Muhammad was convinced that the man was nothing like him and most likely was of the bloody Hindu persuasion.

By the time Mo left the homicide office, the mincing and

grinding of huge amounts of data had confirmed the identity of the man from the brownstone. The suspect went by the name Basil North. The DMV discovered that he held a valid driver's license with a matching photo ID, but owned no vehicle. In addition, he had listed a landline telephone which had never been used for toll calls. He had never been arrested, and no prints or tissue records could be found. The dwelling had been leased in his name for over two years, but was possibly unoccupied until the last eight to ten months. Before that time, Basil North of Washington, D.C., had not existed.

Just as Murray picked up the phone to call JC, dispatch buzzed him on the intercom. They conveyed to him exactly the content of Lauren's call to the station. He promptly barked some orders at them. Then, he flipped through his Roll-a-Dex and quickly dialed her number. She answered on the first ring.

"Chief?"

"I got word from dispatch just now. What's the situation?"

"That same guy made a play at Dr. Thomas' house about twenty minutes ago, looking for that hip part. What's he doing here and what the heck is that thing?" She demanded.

The Chief, overwhelmed by the oddity of the killer's behavior and his appearance anywhere aside from within the apartment being watched, mystified, responded, "I have no idea. What's your status?"

After hearing the Chief's sincerity she calmed down and updated him, "The fugitive is on foot in the area. I think he might have more knives but no gun. JC has superficial wounds…I hear the EMT sirens approaching, now. I don't think we need medical attention but I didn't know at the time. We seriously need some dogs and choppers up here. This guy is dangerous."

"Yeah, K-9 and air units are in route. I don't know what happened with the surveillance team but we're sure as hell going to find out. If Dr. Thomas can make the trip to the station, personally bring him here. We need verification of these images taken earlier this morning and then we're going hunting ourselves—into the lion's den."

As soon as he hung up the phone he proceeded to contact the detectives sitting outside Basil's apartment. They reassured him that they hadn't moved and no one had exited the building. They suggested walking the perimeter to double check and make sure no other outlets permitted departure, though none had appeared on their initial reconnaissance. He instructed them not to move. He did not want anyone encountering this man alone. He also wanted to make sure more than one pair of eyes stood lookout. Other units would come investigate the surroundings.

As he hung up the phone, Chief Lane considered that they might have the wrong man. He definitely needed Dr. Thomas to look at those pictures.

A few minutes before the assistance arrived for the surveillance team, a tiny beige Ford Fiesta pulled up to the back alleyway of the brownstone apartment. With his eyes shifting rapidly, Basil exited the car. Verifying no other person present, he felt secure enough to duck into the alley, slide the empty dumpster aside and return to his lair, just as dawn began to break. This time he looked over at the wall above his desk to check his tracks. A scowl appeared.

At the same time as reinforcements arrived at the apartment. Lauren pulled up to the District Headquarters with JC. She swerved into a parking spot; then quickly escorted him inside the building and into the elevator. She pushed the button for Homicide Department, "3". She asked, "If you don't mind, I'm going to leave you with the people in Homicide while I go and discuss something with Chief Lane in my office before you come down, okay?"

*She's pissed. Somebody dropped the ball but she sure hides it well*, he observed. "No problem, Lauren, but don't get yourself into trouble over me. I'm still in one piece and I got to come with you to work, today. See. Win-win." He felt like any ordeal that allowed him to spend time with her was well worth it--even, near death experiences. His simplicity really tempered her.

She smiled, "Okay. But I do want to find out what happened. And having a civilian there might cause even more tension than already exists."

JC understood, nodded his head and smiled as he exited the elevator on the third floor.

There had been no evidence of anthrax on his last nasal

147

swabs, and everyone at police headquarters had been inoculated anyway, so JC didn't worry about transmitting any lingering bacteria in the building. It was one of the few places he could safely hang out. Once in the homicide offices, JC took his time and was careful to assess the images on the screen. He was certain this was the face he had seen in the predawn hours on the day of the break-in and also at his house over an hour ago. The only difference was that the man on the screen had dark brown eyes. The computer tech slowly altered the color of the iris until JC was finally looking at the same dirty yellow pigment that had burned itself into his memory.

Knowing now that this man had brutally murdered Charlie and two other innocent people and hadn't hesitated to kill JC, the face struck him as even more sinister. Some questions lingered. After the recent encounter it made some sense why he had burglarized the office, and what he was doing near JC's house in the middle of the night Sunday. He was hopeful that the man would soon be caught and could provide some answers to the other troubling questions. *What was that hip implant designed for and who made it?* JC felt encouraged by the progress of the investigation.

Upon leaving the Homicide Division, JC decided to walk down to the second floor, where he found the same sergeant working behind the desk. He noticed there was no playbook this time. Also, the man seemed oblivious to what had just occurred to JC and Lauren.

"Hey, doc, glad you came by. Thanks for the donuts you had sent over this morning. How'd you know exactly what kind we liked?"

*What donuts?* JC thought. *Lauren? That woman thought of everything.*

JC caught completely off guard by the remark quickly recovered. He'd spent a lot of time in the room recovery was named after, tending to post-op patients.

"Just a lucky guess," he said, "and a small bribe for missing curfew the other night. Which I might add was not at all my fault."

The man at the desk stood up and looked down into JC's eyes, "You could have called. But we'll let this slide seeing as how she's in one piece. Plus, she likes you and I like donuts."

JC grateful for both pieces of information he just learned, switched gears, again, "She in by any chance?"

"Oh, yeah, she said to send you right on through whenever you got here."

He knocked. Lauren met him at the door with a kiss and a hug so intimate that he became aware of a lot of things even a well-trained orthopaedic surgeon might not have noticed before.

"John, I was just about to call up for you. I feel better now that the Chief and I got some things sorted out. The next few hours are probably going to be hectic. We both want you under protective custody for a while. That means you're stuck with me here for a bit. When Sanchez's shift is over he's going to take you back home and wait there until I relieve him later today. If you're running low on things, I can pick them up when I come over."

*His face was so refreshingly transparent*, she thought. *I wonder if all surgeons are like that? It could explain why they wear those masks most of the time.* Usually when Lauren encountered people with masks, they weren't in a position to be smiling ear to ear.

"That'd be great," he said. "Anytime, even late would be okay. I don't have any firm commitments for the evening."

"Let's plan on about 7:30," she said before they joined the chorus in unison.

"Unless something urgent comes up."

She continued the thought alone, "If something does come up, Sanchez will stay with you until I can get there."

"Swell," he dryly stated.

A smile stretched across Lauren's face as JC sat down in the chair facing her, but "urgent" was always waiting in the wings.

Back up on the third floor, the Chief wasn't smiling. He knew it was important to move quickly. This guy had brutally killed at least three people in the district and attacked another. He had to be stopped before more innocent lives were lost. He was not likely to be a candidate for rehabilitation. Still, he needed to follow the book. He'd seen people commit horrible crimes before and get off on some technicality. That rule of law was his mandate, and he was careful to follow the bureaucratic procedure step by step.

A judge he had known for years was contacted, and with the help of the prosecutor, an arrest warrant was procured within two hours. In the meantime, he confirmed with the officers on watch that there had been no further comings nor goings from the residence. The additional units had located the secret entrance to the apartment. They had confirmed the apartment's occupancy before closing off the make-shift door in the back alley. They felt the man was alone in the dwelling, but the homes on either side were occupied.

The Chief also alerted the SWAT unit and Hostage Rescue. These highly trained teams were able to review the photos, survey the neighborhood, draw up a plan and move into their concealed positions as the Chief, LB and Tim were arriving on the scene.

Sergeant Dean, the commander of the unit, was a battle-scarred veteran of the military. He would be in charge. One of the first with boots on the ground in Afghanistan, he had selected and rigorously trained his troops for this sort of encounter. Dean also knew from his vast experience that the first plan often went out the window as soon as the enemy was engaged, and he preached the mantra of discipline and flexibility to his men.

Two members of his unit had won long-range distance rifle shooting competitions. These two snipers and their spotters took up positions high on the surrounding buildings. Through the powerful scopes on their weapons, one of the first things the men observed was a tiny security camera moving and pointing at the street from just above the door of the brownstone. The camera hadn't been seen during the night time. The tremendous advantage of surprise was gone. The watchers were already being watched.

Chapter Twenty-six

Some distance away in his office, Pat and several members of his group were working calmly through the crisis. He was buried under the paperwork, but he managed to assign follow-up and coordinating reports on the anthrax event. The search for possibly infected people and the strategy to isolate and treat them was a tremendous resource-consuming task. Hundreds of millions of dollars would be necessary. The legislators who were elected on the solemn promises of lower government spending and better national security in the future would need to make different solemn promises before the next election.

Most of the "unaccounted for" were found, and the ones who weren't probably didn't want to be. Perhaps some of those missing left their families that night to "work late" and accidentally ended up at a basketball game. Perhaps some of them left their families to attend the historic contest, but actually had been attending a different kind of sporting event with their secretaries in hotel rooms which they did not want to become a part of the historic record.

It was likely that a few had made their way out of the arena, not wishing to be held there because of more pressing personal business or political reasons. The FBI could only do so much if people were willing to take their chances for whatever pursuits they deemed more important than life and death.

The decontamination effort went as smoothly as could be hoped under the circumstances. The concentration of spores had chiefly involved the restroom areas, and those were thoroughly cleaned and purged and cleaned again. The latest set of cultures was negative at 48 hours. The arena remained closed to public events, but the surrounding areas had reopened, including the adjacent metro station.

The biggest problem from the public health standpoint continued to be the tracking and treatment of those infected from the first game. The civilian and military hospitals were functioning adequately considering the numbers involved. Their mass casualty protocols were well thought out. They'd learned and modified from the last large unfortunate experience of 11 September.

In the midst of this, there were two bits of good news that Pat presented to the group.

"In spite of the flu epidemic, we have found adequate supplies of appropriate antibiotics for prophylaxis and treatment without tapping our military's reserves. The drug companies have really stepped up to the plate on this one. Cipro will kill the germ if it can get to it in time."

"That's the problem with those big drug companies," the kindly grandmother said. "Those people make so damn much

151

money, but they make such damn good drugs."

The Colonel, who'd spent most of his life leading groups of men into countries that changed their names as often as they changed their governments, replied, "That's the beauty of capitalism, Sweetie. You can go buy some of their stock if you want to."

The grandmother responded to the Colonel with some stock advice of her own. The exact wording of the tip she offered could not be heard by her young grandchildren until they were much older.

"I've just been on the phone with the bioterrorism folks," Pat continued. "It looks like this is a Vollum strain and our immunizations should provide significant protection to the people who had the series."

"Anthrax has been around a long time," said Daniel, the historian of the group, a recovering college professor with previous governmental ties. "Some think that Anthrax was the fifth plague from the Book of Exodus. It infected the livestock, and then their dust caused the sixth, boils on the skin, the cutaneous type. It's also mentioned by the ancient Greek writers.

"It's been one of the favorites for biologic warfare for years now. The first Vollum strain came from England back in the thirties. Unfortunately, there're several mutant strains around now, but the original and easiest to grow was isolated from an infected cow. It can spore up and live in the soil for decades.

"The hard part as a weapon was getting it up people's noses. Back in World War II, the British were really desperate, as we know, and, I'm not making this up, they put it in cow patties and thought about having the RAF drop it behind German lines. They ended up contaminating a part of Scotland while they were playing with that stuff and the area was only recently declared inhabitable again. Both our people and the Russians at least experimented with it in the 50's and 60's. Probably a lot of other folks did too."

Pat declared, "Looks like the people we're dealing with found a delivery system with those silicon implants in the dispensers, and who knows where else. We've got to find the source and find out if there's more out there."

152

"If there is any good news, this particular strain's been around long enough we've studied it and know how to treat it, if we vaccinate or find it early enough."

As the group was digesting that information, the intercom crackled. It was Pat's assistant.

"Pat, I know you said no interruptions, but Dr. Scott's out here from the lab in Virginia and I'm afraid he has a blockbuster that you need to be aware of. He says 'right now'."

Dr. Scott was a scientist with at least two Ph.D.'s and was a man who spent all his time inside a laboratory. While he'd been in charge of portions of the FBI test center for several years, his reports were always routed up thru channels. He never came over to this office unless he was called, and he'd never used the words "right now" to Pat. Within a few minutes, the man and his counterpart from ATF were escorted into the group's meeting room.

Introductions were brief as most of the people knew at least one of the scientists, and Dr. Scott immediately launched into a rather scholarly discussion.

"We have an artificial hip device that was sent over by Murray Lane from D.C. police. It was given to him by a Dr. John C. Thomas as part of a homicide investigation."

"Dr. Thomas?" Pat said. "What homicide?"

"Patient of his named O'Reilly was killed and we believe a prosthesis similar to the one we were given was removed from the man's body. Investigator Lane could give more detail about that. I haven't had a chance to talk to him yet.

"We're not through completely analyzing this, but so far we know that it contains approximately 2 kilograms of uranium 235 with at least a 90% purity factor. As you know, that is way beyond any peaceful commercial grade and could only be used as a weapon. This rod of uranium was rather cleverly encapsulated like a spore inside a solid sheath of titanium-lead alloy which successfully shielded it from detection. We had no blip of gamma or any other radiation emission until we started to cut this for analysis. In fact, this thing could have gotten through any security device that we're aware of. It would have shown up on X-ray as a routine hip replacement."

He stopped to catch his breath and to let the words permeate.

"We don't know the source of the uranium, yet. This weapons grade is so damned expensive to make and requires so much energy that it's almost impossible to hide the production. Therefore, we're pretty sure it's not new. It was so costly to purify for a fission device that it helped sink the USSR economy when they tried to keep up with us. Unfortunately, it's also very expensive to deactivate, and so there was a time after their fall when the Russians said "why bother?"

"It is poorly documented, and while we've tracked a lot of this material, there's always been the worry that some of this was sold through the various mafia factions that took over after the collapse--obviously a very lucrative enterprise. Hopefully, only a small amount of it might exist under the radar.

"Most of what we have here is the dangerous 235 isotope with a little 238 and a very small amount of 234 and 236 which might help ID the origin, but it will take some time to analyze and find the source. I thought it would be better to tell you now."

"Dr. Scott, how much of this do you need to make something like 'The Big One'?" the Colonel asked.

"Good question," said the man from ATF. "Seventy-five kilos traditionally, but it's probably a lot less now depending on how it's handled. Rumor is that our folks out in New Mexico think "suitcase"-sized one of these days.

"I might add that ten kilos probably couldn't be exploded and wipe out a city the size of say, New York, but there are other dirty ways that the irradiation of even four or five kilograms could take a huge bite out of a big apple."

"Gentlemen," Pat said, "We have a lot of work to do very quickly and it sounds like you do, too. Is there anything else we should know right now?"

"One more thing," Dr. Scott said. "The same man that the hip device came out of also had some computer files on his laptop that Dr. Thomas had made copies of before the computer was stolen. From those files on the disc given to us we know O'Reilly had both his hips replaced overseas by a company called Imperial Medical. The files contained information on some of the other patients on the trips as well.

"One named Barbara Jefferson who was a Jane Doe number two in a series of unsolved murders and another girl who lived two blocks from where D.C. homicide found a Jane Doe number three last week. It's been all over the news as a sexual serial killer case. These women were at the same place as O'Reilly at the same time. They went for breast implants. I think we've found your anthrax source and probably Chief Lane's psychopath."

"Pat," he continued, "I can't get through to Chief Lane on the phone, but I bet he'd like to know ASAP."

Pat's boxing instinct to use the left jab to set up the right overhand led him to recognize a classic terrorist attack--create a deadly diversion like anthrax and then come in waves from a different direction. He was already on the phone to the police department while the CIA was talking to Dr. Scott about Imperial Medical. The D.C. Metro's switchboard operator answered on the third ring.

"Metro District Headquarters."

"This is Pat working with the FBI and I need to speak with Chief Lane, please."

The operator was caught a bit off guard. She thought it could be a Federated Bankers Insurance salesman, again. They tried anything to get through. She had her orders, and she liked her job.

"He's out on an emergency and unavailable to take your call. Would you like to leave a message?"

"I'm sorry," Pat said. "Sometimes I mumble. I'm head of counterterrorism for the Department of Homeland Security and this is a bigger emergency. You know, matter of national security."

*Without a secure nation, there would be no job*, she thought.

"He's out on site with SWAT, I'll patch you through."

The Chief answered. It was never good news when Pat called.

"Murray, this is Pat. That hip prosthesis you sent to our lab contains weapons grade uranium. While it has less than what it requires to make a fission bomb that could blow the whole region, it has more than enough to contaminate over a hundred thousand people."

"I'm looking at the suspect's house from across the street right now," the Chief said. "He's inside, and we've got SWAT deployed. He has cameras installed and probably knows we're here, but there has been no contact yet. What do you want us to do?"

"Hold position. I've got federal hostage rescue units in route. We need him alive if possible. This may be our only chance to find out how much of this stuff is in the country and to locate where it's being kept."

"I understand."

"Murray, that disc you sent over with the hip stem strongly implicates this man as the killer of those last two Jane Does in your district, in addition to Mr. O'Reilly."

"Hold on, Pat.... the suspect is calling us from the house right now through our switchboard, you better hurry."

"Try to keep him talking - ETA less than 30."

Chapter Twenty-seven

On an asphalt dappled side-street lined with poorly maintained cars from the last century, the black armored mobile command vehicle of DCPD squatted. The array of squad cars and troopers were huddled around a corner and away from the direct line of sight of the killer's residence. The surrounding neighborhood area had been sealed, and it was clear that there was no longer a serviceable back entrance nor exit to the brownstone. The passageway that Basil had designed on his own and previously used to elude authorities had been secured.

Unfortunately, the adjacent properties had yet to be emptied of their innocent occupants; there was not enough time. The ever present press was cloistered a block away from the front door, and a news helicopter hovered too close above the site and was being warned away. It was early-afternoon, and the cold gray sky was preparing to weep with snow.

Confined in the on-site center, the Chief, LB and Tim, along with the commander of the SWAT unit Sgt. Dean and several technicians, listened to the playback of the message that had just been received.

The officer in charge of negotiations answered when patched through from the same operator at headquarters, but the caller refused to speak with anyone other than the Chief of Homicide. He'd demanded Lane by name. The trace revealed the call to have come from one "Basil North" originating from a brownstone building half a block down the pox-scarred street.

The voice was colder than the weather. It was the same monotone of previously captured psychopaths that the Chief had apprehended over the years who were incapable of remorse. There was a slight accent, maybe British, but the message itself was more chilling than the speaker's voice, even to the battle proven veterans listening.

"I am the one you seek inside the house. I have prepared this building and another one nearby containing children with explosives that only I can render harmless. I demand to be on the television to deliver a message to the infidels of this country."

He continued, "Two members of your press that I shall recognize will walk to forty meters in front of this house and wait. They should bring their microphone and one camera only. They shall remove their outer garments so I can see no weapons. There should be no women present. I will read the message of The Prophet, and then I shall disarm the explosives and surrender to the police who will summon a councilor of the law of my own choosing. You are given fifteen minutes to make these arrangements."

Click.

The recording was analyzed for any sign of weakness in the voice or message, but there was none. They must find anyway to push back, to delay, to find an opening to force compromise. The negotiator returned the call.

"What is your name? We need to talk ... to protect the children. We cannot make these arrangements in the given time ....
"

He was interrupted by the voice.

"I am not stupid. I am mujahedeen. I see the camera. There are many press in the area. You have thirteen minutes until I destroy the first building. I will not talk again unless it is to the

157

press."

Click.

The van was a blur of voices.

One said, "I think he's bluffing ... "

"We know he can't be trusted. We should start evac of the buildings," someone else said.

"First time he sees us move," said another, "he could remote trigger one of these places to kingdom come."

"Smoke and flash ain't gonna work with him potentially hovering over the button."

LB added, "Yes, but if we have innocent children at risk ... "

"Yeah, and the FBI wants him alive."

"Nothing for him to lose, take his chances with the legal system."

The SWAT commander raised his hand for quiet and turned to the Chief.

"Chief, I guess it's your call."

He'd remained silent throughout the exchange. Now he spoke with the firm voice of one used to being in command.

"First, I want every school within two miles to start orderly evacuation. LB, would you start that from the other vehicle, please. We have no choice here except to meet on his terms, but I can't order civilians to go out unarmed and unprotected to meet with this killer."

Sgt. Dean said, "One of us could go, but he'd spot that right away. Best we can do is provide cover."

"This is the biggest news event of the year," Tim said "There's over a dozen reporters down there that I know will volunteer. They all understand the risk. The problem will be to narrow it down to only two."

Time was running out. The Chief knew this was a murderer with very little to lose, and he would not hesitate to kill. He turned to his remaining assistant with renewed confidence.

"Tim, would you go to the press and ask for volunteers of older men, no women. Bring no more than three back here with you and have the patrolmen keep the others confined to our line. Move quickly, please."

"Sgt. Dean," he continued, "Check with your men on the roof. If there's any change in the situation, we need to know. And please remind them, unless there is immediate risk to our people here or the public, we need him alive."

"Yes, sir, right away."

Tim returned with three veteran male reporters who were informed of the details and the obvious risk. They all understood and were willing to go. The Chief picked the two faces that he recognized.

The men removed their coats and sweaters and walked slowly out from behind the cover of the command vehicle. One of the men was armed only with a microphone, while the other awkwardly managed the camera as the pair walked out to the forty meter designated area and waited shivering more from the circumstance than from the cold. The whole scene was a tension filled silent movie filmed in black and white.

Basil observed the proceedings from inside the building. He surveyed the barren room and the empty case. He'd passed all his trophies to Kafeel. It was time for the next step in his plan. He would meet face to face with the infidels. This time, there was no need to cover his eyes.

He stretched and prayed aloud. He then tucked the freshly sharpened large knife in his waist band. It still had traces of JC's blood on it. Then, Basil concealed the smaller dagger at his ankle. Lastly, he placed the vest and the heavy pack on his back just so and threaded his arm through one sleeve of his robe. He turned the gas knob of the stove full on and unbolted his heavy front door.

"Door open," one of the snipers reported to the command vehicle.

Basil went straight toward the spot where the two men were waiting to talk. He walked slowly and with purpose. Before he had covered half the distance, however, he changed his course and started toward the crowd of reporters who were being held back and craning to watch.

"What's he doing?" crackled the radio.

"I don't know, keep tracking him. Maybe he's changed his mind. Maybe he's confused. Tell him to stop."

The two snipers were positioned on the nearby buildings

where they could see the entire area. They were veterans of many battles and had both served in the mountains of Afghanistan and in the deserts of Iraq. They were steady. Their breathing was controlled. Their hands were protected against the cold as they watched and waited for orders.

From the moment the front door opened, these men had closely observed the suspect through their high-powered scopes. They could now see the heavy vest and the pack with a cord emerging from the sleeve to the device in Basil's hand. Any reflex would spring the trigger.

They had seen this walk before half a world away: determined, persistent, and armed. The programmed movements of a deranged robot moving forward like a child's wind-up toy toward an unyielding wall. He was approaching the crowd of civilians and ignoring the pleas from the loudspeaker to stop.

When the killer had progressed to within seventy yards of the crowd, there was no turning back. The snipers knew what they must do.

The "pop-pop" sounds occurred so closely together that it was perceived by the crowd as one noise.

Before the onlookers could see the two bullets enter the head with the yellow eyes or see the crimson stain spurt from each side, Basil released the trigger. The vest and pack exploded with such terrible force and fury that Pat felt it miles away in route. It did not have to be explained to him.

The eruption of the concrete from the street and the metal from the old cars reached the onlookers' souls, but only small bits of the waste touched their bodies. The snipers had reacted in time to prevent serious injury to the crowd of media and bystanders, although the violent shock would leave a lasting image to those present.

Basil North of Washington, D.C., ceased to exist. The pieces were so scattered and so small that it would require microscopic analysis of the tiny mitochondria contained in his cells to even establish a profile of his past identity.

The man, like many others before, was used by his leaders far away for their own ambitions. He was no longer a holy warrior or a proud hunter. He was only a brutal slayer of the innocent, a

160

murderous butcher of defenseless men and women.

His remains would not be carried in a coffin of mourning through the streets. Instead, the small pieces would be swept away, invisible in the wind. It was too late for him to know that there were far more virgins on any street corner in Las Vegas than would be waiting for him in paradise.

Chapter Twenty-eight

The thunderous noise of the explosion faded and was answered by the soulful call of the lone bugle echoing through the purple hills of Arlington Cemetery as the sun set on Wednesday. Pat, who was never chided for slow play in the counterterrorism game, summoned his unofficial group to assemble. Several of the present members had loved ones or comrades-in-arms resting in that hallowed ground across the river, but so far no American lives had been lost from this most recent nuclear threat. Pat was determined to keep it that way.

As with doctors and cops, "urgent" was an irritant that came often and always unplanned in this business of protecting the country from its enemies both foreign and domestic. The hastily called meeting caused the usual disruptions to the schedules of the persons in the group. It was nothing compared to the sacrifices made by the thousands who lay buried across the river, but irritating none the less.

The mystery-writing grandmother had to cancel her investment club research session, and the Colonel had to withdraw from the scheduled poker night with his old friends down at the Russian Embassy. The Chief was trying to take his wife out to dinner to celebrate their anniversary which had come and gone three weeks ago, but he was asked to attend the meeting. In addition, the Chief requested that Lt. Long come along with him to provide the burglary case details which might help shed some further light on the assassin's recent footsteps.

At 7:20, Lauren called JC to explain why she couldn't come over as they had planned. She started and ended with "I'm sorry."

He knew she meant it. He'd been there. All he'd learned from his many last minute excused absences over the years was to try and mute the disappointment.

"An urgent matter of national security at the FBI building sounds a lot more demanding than 'another broken arm in the ER' ," he offered.

"I was really looking forward to our third sort of date," she continued.

"Yeah, so was I, but good grief! Top secret national security issues. When we finally do get together again, we'll have a lot more to *not* talk about."

He heard her smile and felt those eyes twinkle over the phone from miles away before he added, "If you're not too tired, call me when you get through and maybe we can plan something else."

She replied, "Absolutely. And tell Sanchez I told him to get out of your home." She added, "you might want to hand him a pastry as you tell him that, though."

After dismissing his personal offensive line with a bag full of strudels, JC went back to console himself with the distracting TV coverage of Basil's demise. The news channels were getting to be like the neckties that came for Christmas: quite a collection of different styles and colors in the closet, but he only needed one or two for weddings, funerals and court cases. Since he was voluntarily still quarantined at home, he'd get by with cold pizza again tonight, but he was determined he would not set foot in that dusty garage.

At 7:30, the group gathered around a large conference table in their secure room. Pat promptly began with brief introductions of the police officers to the permanent members - first names were all that were needed - and the secrecy of the proceedings was emphasized. He then gave a summary of the radiation risks that were discovered by Dr. Scott in the lab and opened the floor for discussion by saying,

"Okay, we've got a lot of ground to cover and the atomic clock is ticking. Let's start with what we know and what we need to know."

"Sounds to me like we need damage control first," said the non-'Yes man' "Where did these hip prostheses come from and how many more are out there?"

"The original source is unknown," Pat explained. "Dr. Scott and ATF are working up the exact composition of the uranium and then someone will have to get with AEC eventually and go international, but we're not ready to tell the whole world what we know, yet.

"What we do know is that these were put in place overseas by a medical tourism group that goes by the name Imperial Medical. CIA and Interpol will help with the exact location. I believe Dr. Thomas tried to get some info from the hospital they were working out of. It wouldn't hurt to see what he found out."

"How did they get these devices in the country so easily, and how many more have gotten in already?" the Colonel asked.

"We have a disc that Dr. Thomas copied from Mr. O'Reilly's lap top with some of the other patient's personal data. I need someone at State to get with the immigration service and start tracking passport data and trying to match dates. Once we begin to identify some of the remaining unsuspecting patients, we should have a better handle on the magnitude of the problem. Dr. Scott says these things would look like a routine hip replacement on security X-ray with only some subtle differences. Maybe an orthopaedic surgeon could further explain those differences to our screeners."

One of the women said, "Obviously it's going to take some time to find them all. How much danger is there to the public with these things literally walking around?"

"Of course the lives of the people carrying these implants are in danger from other assassins, if they exist," Pat said. "We may have to go public to find these patients before any more can be killed. I understood Dr. Scott to say that as long as the metal device was intact, there was no radiation leak. Now, how easy it is to break one, I don't know. Again someone with experience putting these in might... "

The Colonel interrupted, "Sounds to me like we need somebody with medical knowledge to help us answer some of these questions, but Pat, I don't think even you can find a doctor to come out at this time of night for free who isn't an intern."

As the small amount of laughter subsided, and the assembled looked back and forth at each other, the smallest, most delicate hand in the group was raised. Lauren, from the back row of the class, was not of the nature to be shy or intimidated, but in this group, she was close.

"I could try to call Dr. Thomas if you think that would be helpful."

"Lieutenant that would be very helpful. You will want to call from the secure phone in here, and your doctor should know the call will be monitored," Pat said with a sly smile.

As she dialed, the group tried to be polite, but under the existing laws of biology and human nature, several members developed ear strain trying to not listen to her side of the private conversation.

"Hello, John."

"No, I'm afraid I'm still sitting in a meeting with Pat and his group and this call is being recorded."

"Yes, I'll pass that along to him. Actually, he asked me to call and see if you could come down and help with some of the details and give some opinions about these hip replacements."

She was nodding yes, "Hang on just a minute they're telling me something ... "

"John, he says someone will be at your door in sixteen minutes with a car."

"Yeah ... me too. See you here."

The Colonel who'd spent a great deal of time isolated and alone while crawling across infested jungle floors, said, "Lieutenant, I'm really impressed."

He turned to the grandmother and continued, "Of course, we've still got the anthrax filled breast implants to deal with. You want to see if you can get your plastic surgeon to come on down tonight?"

She politely declined, but volunteered that the Colonel might need to set up an appointment with his Urologist again soon. Fortunately, the exact words of her suggestion would not be heard by her grandchildren until they were much older.

Shortly thereafter, JC was escorted into the room, and before introductions took place, Pat shook his hand and said, "Dr. Thomas, thank you for coming in. You understand, everything that goes on in here is subject to the highest classification of the

National Secrets Act, and we are updating your background check as we speak. That being understood, feel free to listen and talk openly while in this room."

Once he was seated and acquainted, Pat informed him about the uranium in the core of the prosthesis he'd removed from O'Reilly and the updates on the anthrax in the slain women's implants. He spoke slowly, giving JC time to collect himself and comprehend the gravity of the situation. Then he asked about Imperial Medical.

"I got the name and contact phone numbers off of Mr. O'Reilly's laptop before it was stolen from my office," JC said. "I guess Dr. Scott's lab has the copy I made. If O'Reilly had a desktop at home, or you could get his phone records, there might be more information there about the physical location of Imperial."

The Chief and Lauren made affirmative eye contact while JC continued.

"There had been three groups of tourists operated on at their facility over the last two to four months. They sort of rent space to itinerant groups when business is slow. The nurse in charge of the OR said that the hips were put in by a British trained surgeon. If she said his name, I don't remember it, but looking back, I guess it wouldn't have been his real name anyway.

"I hadn't thought of it until now, but she commented on his peculiar yellow eyes. I wonder if he could be family, or at least ethnically related to the man who broke into my office, later tried to kill me, and finally blew himself up?"

"Obviously that man who is no longer a threat, went by the name of Basil North," Pat said, "although that was almost certainly not his name. We will, at some point, have a DNA profile, but as of now we know very little about him."

"Chief," the member from CIA suggested. "We better get all the images you have on your murderer to CIA and start trying to track a doctor somewhere in the world who resembles him."

"I can have those sent over while we're talking if you like," the Chief replied.

"The sooner, the better."

"One or two other things I remember," JC said. "The plastic surgeon was an American named Dr. Moore, and there was a foreign-born dentist - they thought he was Saudi - doing dental implants."

The Chief thought he could soon close the books on Jane Doe number two with the new Saudi teeth, but he still didn't know number three's name. Hopefully the travel records of O'Reilly or Pat would yield that information.

"All of the prostheses were brought into the hospital by Imperial," JC said, "and they were abnormally large and heavy. Now I see why. They show up quite differently on X-ray. We've got some radiographic images at the hospital that I could use to show security screeners what to look for."

"That would be very helpful," Pat said. "JC, the custodian we have, Ali, thought there might have been some activity in Canada. Do you have any thoughts on that?"

JC had a lot of thoughts. During his brief encounter at the basketball game, before Lauren shot the man, JC found that Al was not chatty. *Perhaps Pat's assistants discovered him to be somewhat more of a gossip.*

At any rate he answered, "One of the ways the Canadians have chosen to ration health care is to limit their surgeons' operating room time. I've heard some of them say it can take up to thirty months between onset of symptoms and hip replacement. I could understand a lot of motivation for those poor people to seek services abroad rather than deal with the pain that long."

"Better get some of those X-rays and alert our friends up north as to the possibilities," one of the women said.

"Now, one of the last things for you tonight," Pat said, "is the question of how dangerous are these things and how do we get them out? Dr. Scott says there's no radiation leak as long as they're intact."

"Maybe," JC said, "I could talk to Dr. Scott, but I think any experienced hip surgeon could revise these ... "

Pat had a talent for interrupting without seeming to.

"JC, looks to me like you're the most experienced in the world, having actually done one of these. Would you consider coming to work for us for a while? We're going to need some help on retrieving and exchanging these devices safely, though we don't know how many, yet. In addition, we may well need to go to the

166

news media to alert these people as soon as possible without causing undue alarm to everyone else. I think you could do a great service by helping us on that score."

Dr. Thomas was not often speechless or indecisive. He was not naive, but had he just been offered swamp land in Florida or an old steel bridge to Brooklyn by Pat?

The man previously from ATF spoke, "Since we didn't find any of these weapons at the terrorist's home, I'm assuming he either hid them elsewhere or passed them along. We don't know how many he may have acquired, but we've got to find them, and soon."

"Ali told us about this man named Kafeel- the taxi driver - who was his delivery man," Pat said. "It seems likely that he may be the one who moved these around. Perfect cover driving around the district in a cab. If we can locate him, I'll bet he knows where they are.

"Our people will continue to look for him. We've got a lot of leads, but if he's smart, and I think he is, he's probably already on the move."

After a bit more discussion, Pat said, "I believe we've got plenty to work on. JC, if you don't mind to stay a while, I think we can disperse."

As they were leaving the room, Lauren gave JC a wink, and he thought she could communicate more with the bat of a single blue eye than all the other women he'd ever known put together.

The Colonel had spent a great deal of his life jumping into hostile worlds for the purpose of recon or rescue of hostages. He was an expert on weapons, tactics and leading the unique people of America's Special Forces. He had not majored in political correctness nor graduated from charm school.

On the way out, he approached JC and said, "Doctor, we'll be proud to have you 'on board. I was wondering, would you mind taking a look at my knee sometime? I've been having this catch and I was curious... "

The kindly grandmother took the Colonel's arm and steered him away as she offered some advice on how to behave in certain social situations. They'd been married to each other for some thirty years, but fortunately their young grandchildren would not understand the exact words she used now until they were much, much older.

Chapter Twenty-nine

By noon on the next day it was apparent that the 15-year-old boy who had been exposed to anthrax during the first basketball game would survive. Before the exposure he was healthy and strong, and he would suffer few permanent physical consequences. The emotional scars would take some time to fade. Twenty-seven persons, almost all Americans, died from the terror attack at the stadium, and eighty-four others remained in serious condition.

Congressional investigations were getting under way and were named for the representative who had been exposed. He would also be one of the lucky survivors; his bacteria was diagnosed and treated before it could spread its deadly toxin.

It was fortunate indeed that he was not contagious since it had proved impossible to keep a member of Congress away from the public--whatever germs he carried were aerosolized throughout the nation's capital. The man even made an off the record remark expressing his gratitude toward his physicians and one of the large drug companies. The comment had been caught on tape and made public; he would not be able to retain his seat in the next election.

JC talked with his partners and arranged a temporary leave of absence to work with the FBI on the immediate threat to Homeland Security. The other four doctors in his clinic were very patriotic Americans. They volunteered to pitch in and do the extra work involved to follow his office patients while he was gone and help out with them in any way they could. They were behind him one hundred percent of the way.

Covering his every fifth night on call, however, was a completely different matter. The call schedule was a sacred religious document governed by the rules of generally accepted accounting principles and under more scrutiny than a referee with instant replay. Trades for certain nights could be arraigned, but the total number of nights and weekends for each individual, like pi to the tenth decimal place, could not be altered. When he returned to the practice, JC would have fewer than zero advanced airline miles with his group. Finances and expenses could be arraigned and compensated, but the total number of nights spent on call was strictly non-negotiable.

JC arrived early at the FBI building and was expedited through processing. He shared some time with Dr. Scott and learned a great deal about the anthrax infested breast implants. They discussed the dangerous hip devices in minute scientific detail. They were both terribly concerned with the magnitude of the threat from these weapons and fearful about the consequences they could bring if exploded as dirty bombs. The nationwide security level was at its highest point since the days after 9/11.

JC spent most of the afternoon with the sophisticated electronic data people using O'Reilly's files and matching names with the massive data banks of passports and travel records required to identify the patients of Imperial Medical. If all of the operated patients could not be found or accounted for, then they would have to resort to going public and potentially creating more panic.

Pat felt that JC could best be utilized to help find the people who were walking around on the dangerous implants and then work toward getting them in for removal and revision surgery. He was assured that surgical beds, operating time and the scheduling of cases would be given top priority--it was every well trained orthopaedist's dream come true. He would have all the help he needed, and in spite of the current personnel shortage, available anesthesia would not be a problem.

The task of finding the taxi driver known as Kafeel and the other possible members of the cell would not be JC's concern. In addition, recovering the deadly implants that had already been removed, the number was still unknown, would fall to others who were much more experienced in the tracking and recovery of stolen goods, especially goods utilized as nuclear threats.

He'd worked all day without a break, and by the time darkness fell, things came to a temporary lull. The electronic experts were crunching data, and they estimated that it would be several more hours before anything close to a complete list of patients could be identified.

169

With two full hours of personal time, he reached for the secure phone.

"Hello, Lauren, it's John."

"I wondered ... caller ID said 'Unavailable'. How's it going down there?"

"We're making progress, but I am 'Available.' We've got a couple of hours break while some numbers are being run. How about you?"

"Nothing new to report. I was just about to leave."

"I've got to come back here later, but is there any chance I could meet and buy you a good meal for a change?"

"Chance is near one hundred percent. I'm starving. You pick the place...except no sports bars or pizza places, please."

\*\*\*\*\*\*\*\*\*\*\*\*\*\*\*\*\*\*

Kafeel felt safe with his recent identity change. Once he heard of Ali's capture, he had been aware that the authorities would soon know about him, the taxi driver, the courier, but the janitor did not know the other members of the cell. Kafeel promptly emptied his apartment and abandoned the yellow cab. He had cleared out the rented self-storage unit of the stolen computers, the valuable prostheses and a few other items. They were all resting behind him now in the camper part of the pickup along with a great deal of currency.

The FBI would locate his temporary storage bin very soon, but it would be empty. They could explore his flat and find traces of hair, clothing fiber, prints, and even the DNA of Kafeel, the driver of cabs in Washington. That man was invented only three years ago and now no longer existed.

He'd recently become Mr. Smith, the proud possessor of a green pick-up truck. The previous owner and his wife provided Kafeel with a new life just as their lives ended, and that would not be discovered until their deaths became known. There was plenty of time to transport the weapons that Basil and the other one had collected and to put them in place for the deadly attack.

Then things changed dramatically. Kafeel saw the news. He watched Basil give his life for the cause on a tiny screen in a local cafe. What glory his friend had attained to be killed in the Jihad, a holy warrior, waiting for him to also arrive in Paradise. But the time for them to be joined had not come yet. There was much left to do on this earth to bring down the great Satan. The plan must be again altered.

As he drove the truck south on the small highway, Mr. Smith pondered. How had police discovered Basil? They must know that he'd killed and rendered the hip from the man called O'Reilly. The clues must have been assembled during the day and night that they'd been out of the region collecting the prizes from the woman.

The authorities would soon discover what was contained within the metal core of O'Reilly's other prosthesis, the one stolen by Dr. Thomas. It would not take them long to find the connection between the estate planner and all the medical tourists. If only the foolish American had not broken his leg, the valuable weapon would not have been removed by the doctor. It was certainly in the hands of the authorities by this time. They recognized the threat and raised the alert to red.

The FBI had obtained too many signs now that would lead them to the travel agency, and from there they would soon discover the identities of the other patients. They would search for the remaining tourists and collect them to keep them safe and to purge their bodies. Among the information, they would see Mr. and Mrs. Smith's names and they would soon discover them to be missing and look for the truck. He would have some time, maybe a day or so, but he must, again, shed his skin.

Kafeel carefully thought out a new plan. He could no longer use the papers and passports from the travelers, as many of these identities had been listed in the files of O'Reilly and Imperial Medical. Also, else they could be traced from the remaining patients through the massive computers of the federal authorities. They would be identified, just like the Smiths, so he must not use any of these names for his new identity. He must look elsewhere.

More importantly, he must alert the others. This was not the time to meet at the target and attack as they had planned; the suspicions would be too high. He would store the weapons until the Americans dropped their guard as they always did. Their memory was very short.

Mr. Smith drove the green pick-up further south on the highways knowing he needed to act soon. As night approached, a plan came together. The solution became obvious to him. Sitting behind him in the wooden storage container was the computer from Dr. Thomas's office. He would assume the identity of one of the American doctor's patients. An abundance of names, ages and social security numbers were listed in those files. He could even have a medical history and an HMO insurance policy if he chose.

The approaching truck stop provided the two things he required now: access to the world wide web to warn the others through the doctor's computer and a choice of vehicles in which to continue his journey. He would then hide the prostheses and escape the area. Later he would return after he had become a new person, a person with a previous orthopaedic problem.

Mr. Smith parked the truck in the darkness and went inside the cafe with the stolen laptop. Just as many of the other drivers did during their break, he would enter the wireless world. Sitting unobserved, probably exchanging E-mails with his friends and family, he sent cryptic warning messages through the air to the others throughout the world. This was an emergency. He would later destroy this computer and these few brief notes could not be intercepted by the Americans.

After sending the e-mails he let the battery charge as he lingered over the plate of food. He observed the other people entering the depot. A likely target caught his attention. This careless man appeared to be alone and wore the uniform of a company with a large fleet of trucks. He seemed oblivious to Mr. Smith's presence.

Mr. Smith paid for his meal with cash and left a tip for the waitress. He then retreated to the friendly darkness outside and retrieved the shovel from the camper. It was the same one that Basil had used to hide the couple's bodies in the ground.

As the cold wind blew, Mr. Smith was reminded of the mountain ranges of his home. The large vehicles moved in and out on the other side of the building buying fuel and leaving their vehicles for the lights and comfort of the rest stop. Drivers hurried inside for food and shelter. There were no people out in the parking lot on his side of the cafe.

Patiently, he waited near the truck with the same company name that had been on the man's brown uniform. He noticed several stickers and ribbons on the back of the trailer in praise of American soldiers. He would relish killing this infidel.

The trucker appeared waving goodbye. He laughed and strolled out the door with a toothpick in his mouth and a full stomach. The man was ahead of schedule and looking forward to a nap in his compartment. As he approached and unlocked the door of his cab, the massive force of a shovel suddenly and violently split his head. Before he could even fall, his body was lifted up inside his truck.

With no one around, Mr. Smith, still shielded from the cameras by the trailer, moved the contents of the camper into the truck and started the engine. With a full tank of fuel, he eased out of the parking lot and back onto the highway heading south. He calculated at least twelve hours to hide his stores and abandon the truck before it would be discovered missing. He would have to hurry.

After driving another hour, he found what he'd seen on the map: a safe place where his weapons could be hidden and not discovered until he returned for them. He idled the truck and used the dolly in the trailer to move his heavy wooden container across the path for fifty yards before he dug into the earth for a few feet.

The box was some four feet long but only two feet high and two feet across. It was easily large enough for all the nuclear prostheses, the remaining anthrax containing implants and the stolen computers from which he'd copied the doctor's files, but the hole would not need to be too deep. The contents inside his crate were packaged in several waterproof containers. Like spores, they would lay beneath the soil, protected until they were summoned forth to spread death and disease.

After driving for another two hours, Mr. Smith abandoned the truck in a roadside park and set out on foot across a mountain with his backpack. Inside the pack were a few computer discs and the patient information needed to create dozens of new identities. He also carried American currency alongside his dagger which rested in its sheath.

By the next morning, while Seth Rogers was making his way to Dr. Thomas's office to have his cast changed, Seth Rogers was also picked up by another member of the sleeping cell in a small city hundreds of miles away from Washington, D.C. By changing names and by differing modes of transportation, Kafeel as-Hamid, Mr. Smith, and various other identities the courier had adopted, would disappear on a long trip west and take a short vacation. He was convinced that things would go smoothly for him on his journey. After all, he was accompanied by a friend who had a great deal of experience in the travel industry.

Chapter Thirty

Lauren smiled as she walked into the restaurant. She was under the impression that she could tell a lot about some people by what they chose to eat for dinner and by where they selected to eat it. The place that JC suggested was not the most expensive only-go-once-a-year-for-your-birthday type, but it was exclusive enough to make her feel special.

Forget the guide books, this was where the Cattleman's Association met when they came to Washington. They had the best steaks in town. It was classic American fare: red meat with stripes of white marbling and ranch on the salad.

JC was already seated, but he got up and came forward to meet her in case she didn't recognize him in the dim light. The thought flashed through his mind that it would almost be worth getting arrested just to see her smile. She, on the other hand, didn't notice the wear in the old blue blazer or the neck tie from a Christmas past. He could have been wearing an orange jump suit and flip flops as far as she was concerned. Most of the cattlemen looked up and saw the two meet, then turned to their wives and grinned like teenagers with their braces recently removed.

They sat down next to each other close enough to touch and looking forward to an uninterrupted hour or so of each other's company. Almost on cue, as the waiter poured the water, Police Lieutenant Long's office cell phone chimed in and her smile faded.

After a minute of listening, the smile was back and even brighter. It occurred to JC that there was one subtle difference in their professions. The nurses never called him to say that the patient had taken an unexpected turn for the better. Lauren indicated "come with me" as she pulled him closer to the phone, and the two of them retreated toward the lobby to a small private alcove. Once out of earshot of the other diners who were enjoying their sizzling primes and loaded baked potatoes while avoiding the obligatory sprouts of steamed broccoli, she introduced JC to the caller.

"John, it's Eric, one of our tech people. Those computers that were taken from your office apparently had a program installed by your data consultants. When we reported them stolen on the day of the break-in, a service you contracted with sent up an electronic red flag. One of those laptops just went on line for the first time and your service is backtracking the packets of data coming along the route. In a few minutes they say they can come close to the physical location of your machine by identifying which network he's working from."

By then she had switched to speaker so JC could both hear and talk.

"Eric, this is JC Thomas. Will the operator of that laptop know we're looking over their shoulder?"

"Probably not. It wouldn't even show up on the systems contained list except as a line of some cryptic characters."

Eric paused then spoke again, "There is one thing. This company can electronically erase your files to protect you from his getting in and copying everything in there. If they start to wipe it clean, and if he knows anything about computers, he would probably get real suspicious real fast and shut down, in which case they would lose him."

"You mean they can continue to track him as long as he stays connected or every time he comes on line?"

"Basically that's correct unless he knows enough to wash the hard drive or we do it for him. Hang on, they're asking me whether you want them to start erasing now or not."

JC knew exactly what to do for a dislocated ankle and a fractured femur. He was confident taking care of a torn knee ligament or a severely bleeding arm. He had years of training and experience. But now he was looking at a completely different problem. He could risk giving private sensitive information on thousands of unsuspecting people to deadly terrorists or continue to have some chance to discover the radicals' whereabouts. It was his first big official decision and he'd only been on the job for twelve hours.

"Do not erase. Keep tracking and tell them that law enforcement will call them right back." Hopefully Pat could keep him out of jail for aiding and abetting all kinds of HIPA violations.

Before Lauren could flip her phone off, JC was on his cell to Pat, and it took less than a minute to quickly repeat the conversation.

"Good move, JC. We'll get started on the electronic tracing while you make your way back over here. Oh, and would you see if Lt. Long can come with you? She seems to have the best handle on your burglary case."

*******************

Hamilton Bates had processed data for the service that tracked missing computers for eleven months, which coincided with the last time he'd actually been seen outside in the daylight. The blinking screens and flashing lights were like colorful ornaments for him. The whole world was there waiting for his click from inside the windowless room.

It was part of his job to alert the company's clients when there was electronic evidence of a stolen computer being used. From that point on, it was up to the local law enforcement people if they chose to pursue. It had been his experience that the police usually had enough to do without bothering to try and retrieve one machine.

"We'll call you right back" ... yeah ... sure ... they never called right back. The familiar mantra was going through his head even as his extension began to buzz. When he toggled the earpiece on, Hamilton Bates spilled most of his mocha java with the triple shot and barely missed soaking his keyboard.

"Ham, this is the headquarters of Homeland Security. This is a national emergency. Stay on the line and plug me into your data stream on the missing Thomas computer."

Pat then gave the MAC code identifying the specific laptop, but Hamilton Bates could type faster than he could listen, and he was already pushing "Enter".

It took fifteen minutes for JC and Lauren to return through the back door of the heavily guarded building. They forgot about being hungry. The waiter understood. It happened all the time in Washington.

The guard at security was alerted, and Lauren's Official Visitor Pass was ready by the time she had checked her weapon. They were escorted straight up to the secure meeting room where the rest of Pat's informal group had gathered. They entered the room to hear Pat mid-sentence,

"The data information techs traced a stolen laptop to a Wi-Fi spot at an interstate truck stop two states south. The local sheriff and highway patrol are fifteen minutes away from reaching the area, and the Special Agent in Charge of the nearest field office, Shauna Owens, is on the line while heading to the location.

Due to the time interval between alert and trace, the last signal had been received over an hour ago, but Hamilton Bates and the FBI were still listening for a ping. Once the cavalry arrived at the roadside stop, the place was sealed. No person and no vehicle went in or out. Everybody, including the cooks, cashiers, truckers in the showers and anyone sleeping outside in the cabs, was identified and brought inside the cafe. Interviews were being conducted and the security camera tapes from the parking lots were being reviewed.

Within thirty minutes of their arrival, every vehicle present at the time of the first electronic hit could be accounted for except the one green pickup truck with a camper shell on the back. It would not take long to trace its registration back to Mr. Smith, the same Mr. Smith who was known from O'Reilly's files, to have been "very interested in estate planning."

The waitress recalled serving a man who'd paid in cash and left without his receipt. She'd wondered at the time if he was a driver. He had seemed intent on his computer, didn't talk to anybody, and her recollection of his appearance was rather vague. He'd probably been gone for over two hours by now.

The tractor-trailers that had departed over the last two and a half hours were identified, and the remaining teamsters were giving information on them. Many in the group knew each other and they were all watching the surveillance videos from the parking lot.

Bob Green had driven for First National Trucking for fifteen years. He saw the tape of another FNT truck that had turned south out of the lot an hour and fifty minutes earlier.

"Hold the phone! I just followed Hank up here from Florida en-route to Baltimore. We were gonna get a few hour nap and continue on together. His rig's leaving out the wrong way. It should be headed north. Something's wrong. He doesn't make that kind of mistake."

The SAC relayed that information to the secure room in Washington where most of Pat's group was assembled and listening over the speaker. Amid the general buzz of conversation from the room, a call was put through and the dispatcher at First National Trucking answered his outside line.

"FNT dispatch, this is Richard."

"Richard, listen carefully," Pat said with calm in his voice. "This is Homeland Security. We're in the middle of a significant terrorist threat and I need your help. We believe one of your rigs on 1-95 has been stolen and is transporting dangerous material."

"That would explain a lot. GPS tracking is showing a truck going the wrong way. I've tried to make contact with the driver for a little while. He won't answer us."

"Can you tell me where he is and where he's been?"

"It's coming up on screen now. You guys got a map down there?"

"Yes and I've got my finger on the truck stop. What have you got from there?"

"From that stop, he went South on the interstate for twenty-one miles and turned west on State Highway 521."

"I follow you, then what?"

"After thirty miles he turned north for a mile on a two lane and idled for forty-six minutes. Then he double backed to the state highway and continued west another thirty miles. He shut the rig down and it's still sitting in a road side park three miles over the mountain as the crow flies from the town that you see there on your map."

"Richard, can you stay with him and let me know if he moves an inch?"

"Roger that ... 1 can tell you if his oil pressure drops."

Pat returned to the special agent, "Shauna, did you get that?"

"Loud and clear."

"I want you to follow to the idle point and call me when you arrive. Could be radiation or biological weapons involved. Take precautions, but hurry. I'm going to send another, closer team to the end point at the roadside park."

Within thirty minutes, the second team reported back. They had found the First National rig abandoned in the roadside parking lot. The cab was empty except for the body of its former driver who appeared to have died from a massive head injury. Resting beside him was a dirty, blood-stained shovel.

Forty-five minutes later, shortly after midnight, Agent Owens called to say her crew was at the point where the truck was known to have idled.

"Shawna, what are you seeing?"

"It's eerie really. The moon just came out from behind the clouds and the wind has picked up. Hope you can hear me okay. We're looking out over a large cemetery with one ... two ... three fairly freshly dug graves."

It didn't take long for the group to realize it was the ideal hiding place.

"Agent Owens, start digging into the freshest...cautiously. Put us live on your video feed and let me know when you hit something."

After several minutes of digging, as observed by the group on the grainy camera feed, a wooden box was discovered to be sitting on top of an underlying casket.

In the darkness, it was difficult to see clearly as the crate was opened, and the vague images being transmitted were interpreted differently dependent on each member's point of view and past experience.

To Pat, it looked like a cache of nuclear and biological weapons. One threat to the nation had been aborted, but vicious terrorists were still loose in his country. It was halftime and the score was still tied.

To the mystery-writing grandmother of the group, the area looked like the deserted English moors and the treasure in the wooden chest could have been a priceless diamond necklace or perhaps a jewel encrusted black falcon from Malta.

JC and Lauren saw as one--some recovered stolen goods and some defective hip prostheses. There would be a lot of orthopaedic work to do after the other patients could be found, but for now there would be a weekend away from the city for the two of them. When they returned to Washington on Monday, spring would come and the cherry trees would be resplendent with the pink blooms of peace.

The historian and former professor in the group relapsed when he saw the image and began to pontificate. To him, the crate symbolized another wooden structure with dangerous contents, a giant horse that had been brought inside the walls of a great city near the end of the Bronze Age, just before men learned to make more powerful weapons.

Epilogue

As the peroxide of time bleaches the ink of history, it becomes harder to know whether the legend becomes truth or the truth becomes legend. Throughout mankind's poorly recorded past, people have often built new cities on top of the remains of older settlements. When it comes to real estate, a good location seems to have eternal value.

On the edge of the ancient Persian world, in a country we now call Turkey, can be found such a site with many layers. Archeologists that have excavated this region feel that one of the deeper levels corresponds to the fabled city of Troy--chronicled by Homer and other classic authors. By some historians' accounts, the city was called "Ilium" after one of its founding sons.

Ilium, is also the name given to the largest bone of the pelvis, the one that provides most of the support required to anchor the socket component of a total hip replacement.

Made in the USA
Lexington, KY
23 February 2012